The Sara Colson Trilogy

Book Two : Sara's Loss

By

Susan Elle

For

Ursula Publishing UK

Sara's Loss
Text Copyright © 2012
by Susan Elle
for Ursula Publishing UK
All Rights Reserved

Cover Photograph
© Sebastian Czapnik/Dreamstime.com

ISBN 978-1-910753-01-9

Other Books by Susan Elle

The Sara Colson Trilogy
Sara's Child
Sara's Loss
Sara's Shame
All the above also available as audio books.

Catherine Colson-Sayers Investigations
(CCS Investigations)
Book 1 : Missing
Book 2 : The Chosen
Book 3 : Travis
Book 4 : Deleted

Tempest
Broken

Love, Lies & Consequences Trilogy
Book One : Love
Book Two : Lies
Book Three : Consequences

Langdon Trilogy
Heart & Home
Heart of a Lion
Heart of Stone

http://www.susan-elle.com

Table of Contents

Chapter One

Caroline Thornton, pianist extraordinaire has just performed her last concert of a mini tour in Ireland, the land of her dad's ancestors. Standing tall and regal in a long scarlet silk dress, she takes a bow, curtsying first to the left and then to the right, then blowing a kiss to the rapturous applause of the audience.

Her smile is broad, though she is exhausted by the effort she puts in to every performance. "Ellisa, did it go well?" Caroline asks her PA as she takes the glass of iced water that always awaits her in the wings after every performance.

"You were perfect, as ever," Ellisa beams, "and the audience loved you."

"Is my dad here?" They walk quickly to the dressing room, which is filled with flowers. "Oh, how lovely."

Caroline walks to each bunch, reading the cards and handing them to her PA for her attention later. "My dad," Caroline turns to Ellisa, "is he here?"

"Yes, he was a bit late due to traffic," Ellisa smiles warmly, "you know he never misses a performance. I bet he's just struggling to get back-stage through all your admirers."

Her grin widens and Caroline continues to smell all the lovely flowers and read the cards. "Oh...this one's from Clive." For a moment, she touches the red roses with a gentle hand. *Why, Clive? I love you so much. Why wasn't I enough?* Remembering their last night together, Caroline squeezes her legs together in an unconscious effort to stop her body reacting to the memory of Clive's hands on her.

He always knew how to arouse her. Fast and hot, her responses had always been like that. He only had to look at her to get the spark to flare in to flames. But when he put his hands on her, when his lips found her breasts and tugged at her nipples with just the right mix of pleasure and pain she could orgasm even before he was inside her. But she wasn't a selfish lover, she had pleasured him too. Had loved to listen to him groan with the pleasure she gave him. *Why, Clive? Why wasn't I enough?*

Picking the bouquet up, Caroline hands them to Ellisa with tear filled eyes, "get rid of them, please."

Taking the offending roses, Ellisa turns to the dressing room door just as it opens and Caroline's dad walks in. His expression goes from proud, adoring dad to one of a concerned parent at the sight of his daughter in tears.

"What on earth's going on?" He looks from his daughter to her PA, but Ellisa just frowns down at the roses in her hands and shakes her head, and then takes them away. "Caroline...?"

"Oh, dad!" With that plaintive cry she flings herself in to her father's arms and cries because her heart is broken. *Thank god I have you, dad. My lovely, lovely, dad.*

Tom allows his daughter to cry whatever it is out of her system then guides her over to the small settee and sits with her. "Tell me..." and hands her his handkerchief, "...what is going on?"

"Oh, dad!" After wiping her eyes and blowing her nose, Caroline looks up at her dad and her bottom lip trembles pitifully.

"I got that bit already," he chucks her under her chin and gives her an encouraging smile, "now tell me what's upset you – was it something to do with those roses Ellisa was taking out?"

Caroline nods. "They were from Clive," she mutters miserably. *Why couldn't he have been like you, dad? So strong and reliable. So loving.*

Closing his eyes and taking a deep calming breath, Tom growls as his temper spikes. "That selfish good-for-nothing, I hope you're not thinking of taking him back — he doesn't deserve you after what he did!"

Shaking her head, Caroline leans against her dad. "Why did he do it, dad? I thought he loved me..." *Am I such a bad person? Don't I deserve to be loved?*

"He doesn't know what love is to behave like that," and Tom remembers his Sara, how much he loved her and how broken he'd been when she had insisted on a divorce. "There's someone better than him out there just waiting to meet you," he encourages. "And when you do, you'll realise that Clive is nothing, and that what he gave you was a very poor imitation of love." Tom's voice becomes wistful. "Real love lasts a lifetime, if tended properly." *I wish I knew what I did wrong, Sara.*

Back at their hotel, Ellisa runs Caroline a bath with her favourite scented oil added. "Can I order you some supper for after," she asks, concerned that Caroline hasn't eaten properly since she found out about Clive's philandering a month ago. And she is losing weight she can ill afford to, in Ellisa's opinion.

"No, thanks, Ellisa," and tries to smile but fails miserably. "I think I'll just turn in after a good soak. See you in the morning." Food. No way!

Clive climbs in to bed beside Caroline, kissing the nape of her neck and trailing his soft lips up to her ear. "You taste hot," he murmurs as his teeth nip and his tongue pushes into her ear.

"I didn't think you would come," she tells him, turning over to kiss his adventurous mouth. Lifting her chin she feels his tongue and teeth nip and tease their way down to her breasts. She's already on fire for him, and arches her back when he draws her nipple deep into his mouth and tugs in just that crotch tingling way he has. His hand moves to caress her other breast while his mouth continues to devour and delight her.

His fingers and teeth tug at her nipples then roll them in turn, a rhythm that drives her wild and over the edge just as the long fingers of his other hand plunge in to her. She screams his name as he pumps his fingers, dragging out the orgasm until she is gasping for air.

"Always a pleasure." Clive gives her a cocky smile then moves his lips to kiss her navel, then slowly moves down to her still throbbing sex. He takes the bead of her sex between his teeth and tugs gently, licking his tongue over her driving her insane with pleasure.

"Clive...please..."

"Please what...tell me?"

She's aching so deep inside, desperate to be filled by him. "Inside me, please, Clive. I need you inside me."

He gives a wicked laugh, and instead of moving over her he moves down and plunges his tongue inside her making her cry out in pleasure. Working her with expert ease, he brings Caroline to the brink then moves over her and plunges deeply, forcefully inside her.

Her gasp of surprise and pleasure drive him on and she meets his punishing pace beat for body slamming beat.

"Yes, yes...aahh" she screams as her body explodes around him and he rears up to plunge once more, hard and deep, as he too gains a powerful release. "Oh christ, Jenna...christ!"

Sitting up in her bed, Caroline sobs at the dream that was so real it is tearing her in two. That was how she'd found out about Jenna, and eventually all the other women Clive had been playing around with.

Wrapping her arms tightly around her, Caroline falls back on her pillow and sobs herself in to a thankfully dreamless sleep.

Walking into her flat, Caroline breathes a huge sigh of relief to be home. "Oh, Ellisa..." Caroline holds her arms out wide and does a twirl in the middle of her sitting room, "...you know, the best part of going on tour is the coming home." Her smile is huge as she flops down on one of the large cream leather settees.

"You've got a lot of post; do you want me to get straight on to it?" Ellisa crosses the sitting room while flipping through the many envelopes she has picked up from the hallway.

"Ok, you do that and I'll unpack." Taking her cases through to her bedroom, Caroline heaves the big one on to the bed. *Crikey!* Taking out the performance gowns, she hangs them up on the back of her bedroom door, ready to be sent to the cleaners.

Working quickly, Caroline soon finishes sorting her own unpacking and heads back through the sitting room to get Ellisa's suitcase. But as she crosses the room she notices Ellisa frowning over a letter, a look of concerned concentration on her face.

"What is it, Ellisa?"

"I...I..." looking up at Caroline, Ellisa's eyes are round and nervous as she regards her employer and very good friend, "...Oh, Caroline."

Filled with concern, Caroline closes the short space between them and takes the letter that appears to have caused her PA such distress.

Her face pales and her legs give way beneath her, leaving her sitting on the honey coloured carpet looking stunned up at Ellisa. *No. No. No. This isn't real. It can't be!*

Moving quickly, Ellisa puts a hand under Caroline's elbow and helps her to her feet then guides her to the settee. "I'm so sorry, Caroline – I didn't know what to do." Watching her boss, Ellisa tries to gauge her reaction to the contents of the letter. "Do you think it's true – or perhaps someone is playing a cruel hoax?"

Head shaking slowly, Caroline lifts the letter and reads it again.

Dear Ms Thornton,

I wish there were a more sensitive way to impart this delicate information, but I have racked my brains and come up with nothing.

I understand you work closely with your father, Thomas Thornton, and that he travels with you on your tours. From this I would have to assume that you are close, and therefore may already be in possession of the facts to which I will now refer. However, as you have never made contact with Catherine I will also assume that this is not the case and will try to impart this information as sensitively as a letter allows.

My fiancée's name is Catherine Colson, daughter of Sara Colson. Her mother was murdered in a most horrific manner, all of which she witnessed. As you can imagine, this caused Catherine a good deal of trauma. So much so that she began her own investigation in to her mother's death and, subsequently, was instrumental in the capture and incarceration of the man responsible.

It was during this process that Catherine mentioned her father. Someone she had never met and did not even know his name. I am afraid it was my own curiosity concerning her father that revealed your existence.

Catherine will be twenty-six on 15th July, as will you I believe. I was looking for her father, Mr Thomas Thornton, married to Sara Colson, and was surprised to find a sibling. I realise that, if you are not already aware of Catherine's existence, this news will come as a shock. I am hoping that once you have assimilated this information, you will want to meet your sister.

For this reason, I have enclosed two first class return tickets in the hope that you and your father will use them to visit with us. We will be very happy for you both to stay with us at our home and will pick you up from the airport should you decide to come.

I do hope that you will forgive the shocking nature of this letter and consider the invitation to visit most carefully and with an open heart.

Yours, most sincerely

Mr Logan Sayers

On behalf of Catherine Colson

Tears trickle slowly down Caroline's pale cheeks. "How could my dad hide this from me?" Her hands are trembling as they fall in to her lap, still clutching the terrible letter. Getting to her feet, Caroline begins to pace the sitting room. "He always got upset when I asked about my mother, so I gave up. But I never dreamed...I had no idea..." *Why didn't he tell me? Why were we kept apart? Why...*

Watching her friend's torment is agonising for Ellisa. There is nothing she can do to lessen the blow Caroline has been dealt. First Clive turns out to be a lying cheat, and now the father she idolises... Well, deceived is too mild a word for what he has done to Caroline, and Ellisa feels angry on her behalf.

"Please, Caroline, let me get you something..." she offers desperate to do something useful, "...a glass of iced water, or a cup of tea, perhaps?"

Looking at Ellisa as if she is speaking an unknown language, Caroline stares blankly then shakes her head. "I need to phone my dad. I need to get to the bottom of this." Her voice has grown stronger, but Ellisa can see the trepidation in Caroline's eyes.

"I'll take the rest of the post through to the office," Ellisa says, and crosses the room to pick up the pile of letters. Turning to look at Caroline, she frowns at her uncharacteristic hesitation. "The best way is to get it done quickly – you'll only torture yourself otherwise." Then Ellisa makes her way to the office to give Caroline her privacy.

Taking Ellisa's advice, she picks up the telephone and calls her dad. But when he answers she is too choked up to speak.

"Caroline...is that you...?" *Why, daddy, why didn't you tell me?* Her dad sounds anxious, but still she cannot answer. "Caroline, please, if that's you, just take a deep breath and answer me." He can hear someone crying quietly at the other end of the phone ine, and it's tearing him apart. "Ok, sweetheart, I'm coming over. Just you sit tight."

At any other time Caroline would have been happy and eager to see her dad, her idol in so many ways. Listening to the drone of the disconnected call, the phone still on in her lap, Caroline presses the end button and replaces it in the cradle.

Her tears increase and, letting the letter fall to the floor, she curls in to herself on the settee.

When the doorbell sounds ten minutes later, Caroline is still curled up on the settee, but her tears have finally dried. Knowing that Ellisa will get the door, she tightens her arms about her not able to look at her dad, the one man she has trusted her whole life.

Closing her eyes tight, Caroline tries to cut herself off from the mumbling voices in the hallway, dreading this confrontation with her dad.

Tom bends, picking up the discarded letter he reads it then sits down heavily at Caroline's feet. "Christ, Caroline..."

WHY! WHY! WHY! Her head is splitting with the thoughts screaming around in her head. *Please, tell me there's an explanation for all this - that you didn't lie to me, daddy.*

Pushing his hands back through his raven hair, Tom regards his daughter, huddling herself up against the world – against him. "I'm so sorry, Caroline..." he watches her eyes screw up even tighter and her bottom lip tremble, "...I never dreamed you would find out this way." He sighs heavily, looking down at the letter in his hand.

"So it's true," she whispers tonelessly. "You're just like Clive, all the secrets and lies."

I don't have anyone left. Nobody I can trust!

"No, Caroline, it was never like that," Tom exclaims, hurt by her accusation. "Your mother wanted a divorce; I didn't have any say in it. And as you were always so attached to me and Catherine to her mother, that's how we agreed to keep it." He moves to touch her, just to lay a comforting hand on her calf, but withdraws it when she flinches away. "Sweetheart, it wasn't my choice."

Caroline sits up and away from her dad, scrunching herself up in the corner of the settee. "So you say." She can't bring herself to look at him. "You can't even say my mother's name, you never have. Why is that, dad?" Caroline's voice has gone from bewildered to accusatory, and her spine has stiffened as she forces herself to look at him. *What did you do to make her want to divorce you? Did you lie? Cheat. Both.*

His eyes are damp, but Tom squeezes the emotions back, swallowing down his pain. "I loved Sara with all my heart," he says, regarding his daughter's steely blue eyes with heavy sadness. "I've never stopped loving her. I'd give anything to know the why of it, but she's gone and there's no one left to ask." His voice is monotone, but the hurt running through it is unmistakable.

Seeing her usually strong father with his shoulders slumped, his head bowed over the letter, Caroline can't bear to see his pain. Getting up from the settee she moves to sit closer to him and puts her arm through his and hugs him. "I don't understand, but I can see that you're hurting too. I just wish you had trusted me, had told me all of this yourself, instead of keeping secrets."

He pats her hand on his arm. "I'm sorry, Caroline, but your mum thought it was for the best. And I was too much in shock to disagree with her." Tom shakes his head in wonder. "It seemed to make sense at the time – she thought you would both end up pining for each other if you knew. So we agreed on a clean break. I moved away to make it work, and because I couldn't bear to see her. Just the thought of her with someone else..."

"Oh, dad!"

First class on an aeroplane is certainly comfortable, Caroline observes as she takes her seat. Looking out over the tarmac, her thoughts drift back to her father. He made some excuse about needing to look over some performance requests and contracts that couldn't wait, but she knows he just isn't ready to face Catherine. To face his past in Sheriton.

Taking a deep breath Caroline settles back for the flight and just hopes that by the time she lands she will be ready to face Catherine.

Waiting at the carousel for her luggage, Caroline reaches out to take one suitcase as it nears then waits for the second. A couple of minutes later she has them both settled on a trolley and begins wheeling them through to the arrivals lounge.

Stopping to calm herself, Caroline realises how nervous she really is. Her heart is racing and her chest is tight. She hasn't felt this nervous since her first ever opening night. *Lord help me. I hope this isn't a huge mistake.*

Caroline realises that she's more than nervous – she's terrified. *Maybe Catherine is too*, she rationalises. *She doesn't know me either – what will she be expecting. Jesus, I hope she's not the hugs, kisses and floods of tears type.*

Pushing the luggage trolley, Caroline rounds the corridor into arrivals – and sees herself staring shocked and amazed back at her. *God almighty!*

She has my face. Her mind spins and she leans on the trolley for support, then forces her feet to move forward. *She has my face.*

As she nears Catherine it is she who wants to cry, to hug her sister hello. But she holds herself in check – her sister may not welcome that kind of intimacy so soon.

It is Logan who breaks the tenuous silence. "Caroline…welcome. Let me take your luggage," and he reaches over to take the two large suitcases from the trolley. Both women are still staring in shock at the other, both mesmerised by their identicalness.

Caroline recovers first, and holds out a trembling hand to her sister. "Hi," is all she can manage to say.

Catherine stares at her hand and Logan fears she will turn away. But slowly, Catherine takes her sisters hand. "Hi."

Letting out a breath he hadn't realised he was holding, Logan invites Caroline to follow him out to the car. *So far so good!*

Both women follow in silence, glancing furtively at each other.

In the car Catherine gets behind the wheel of her brand new car, despite Logan's offer to drive.

Caroline sits in the back, refusing Logan's offer to take the front seat. She's no more ready than Catherine to force this meeting along any faster than the dead slow pace it has taken thus far.

Caroline studies her sister, so capable and confident in her driving - but she doesn't think that confidence goes very deep. For some reason Caroline finds herself feeling sorry that she wasn't with Catherine when she endured their mother's death. The thought of her in foster care makes Caroline angry and sad. Why hadn't their dad brought her home to live with them? Was it because he'd never told her about her sister – her identical twin sister?

Yes, they had to be identical twins – she gazes up to the rear-view mirror and finds herself looking directly into her own eyes and both women gasp as one. *Shit!*

The drive back to Sheriton is short. They arrive at Logan's house and Mrs Baines welcomes Caroline; managing to hide her shock she tells Caroline that she has made a room up for her. And when she protests that she already has a room booked at a local hotel, Logan dismisses the idea.

"You're very welcome to stay with us for as long as you want." Then he carries her luggage up to her room.

Catherine follows Mrs Baines into the kitchen but carries on, out to the large conservatory. As well as a six-seater dining table the conservatory has comfortable seating arranged near the curved window wall with small tables dotted in between. Now what!

Caroline follows behind, admiring the lovely house and furnishings - obviously expensive but comfortable and homely. When she follows Catherine in taking a seat at the far end of the conservatory, she is stunned by the lovely view.

"What a wonderful garden." Caroline turns a smile on her new-found sister. "Could we go for a walk outside?" *Maybe you'll actually speak to me.*

Catherine turns to Logan as he enters. "I'll just get the key," he smiles at Caroline, and turns a questioning frown on Catherine.

Both women remain silent, waiting for Logan to return. Caroline looks out over the expansive grounds, Catherine looks at her sister.

When Logan returns and unlocks the French doors, Caroline thanks him and steps out in to the glorious sunshine and fills her lungs with the clean country air.

Logan gives her a warm smile, admiring her grace and poise, the peach coloured summer dress swirling gently around her knees in the soft breeze. When he turns back to Catherine she is frowning darkly, watching him intently. "Catherine...weren't you going for a walk, too?" He really isn't sure what to make of her reaction to this situation and only hopes that he's done the right thing.

Standing awkwardly, Catherine moves to the open doors and follows Caroline as she heads off to explore the grounds.

Logan turns concerned eyes to Mrs Baines who's been watching the scene play out from the kitchen. "Give her time. Give them both time." She advises sagely, and Logan nods, turning back to watch both women walk in silence until they move out of sight.

<u>Chapter Two</u>

The overgrown pergola comes in to view and Caroline heads for the sheltered seating area. When Catherine doesn't sit, but stands to one side scuffing the toes of her shoes in the dirt, Caroline sighs quietly.

"You're not happy that I'm here." Her voice is quiet, and a little sad.

Catherine frowns down at her feet, and then looks cautiously up at Caroline. "Truth be known, I don't know how I feel," she states then looks back down at her feet. "I didn't know you were coming till this morning. And I didn't know..." Catherine looks up, her face an open book of raw emotion and uncertainty.

"You didn't know that we we're identical...?" Catherine nods, and Caroline smiles ruefully. "Same here." And when Catherine's head shoots up to look at her, continues, "I got the shock of my life at the airport. There I was, looking at myself, looking as shocked and as scared as I felt inside. If it weren't for the luggage trolley I swear, I would have keeled over."

Catherine nods her silent agreement, remembering how her knees felt shaky and her breathing had become so difficult. "Logan said he invited your dad to come with you."

Frowning, Caroline regards her sister, trying to work out why she is being so distant. So...tightly restrained. "Please sit with me," she pats the seat next to her and smiles when Catherine complies. "He's your dad, too. Don't you want to ask me about him?"

But Catherine only shakes her head, and Caroline realises that she is going to have to be the one to take the initiative if they are ever going to get to know each other. *He loved you, too. And he will again.*

"Can you tell me why not?"

Suddenly Catherine stands up, frowns angrily at Caroline and says, "I don't have a dad. I've never had a dad. So, no, I don't want to hear about your dad. Ever!" With that she turns and runs back to the house, leaving Caroline stunned and deeply wounded.

But she has seen the depth of hurt in Catherine's eyes; has seen the tears that she could barely hold in check.

Continuing her walk around the grounds, Caroline determines to find out more about her sister. What has hurt her so badly, and what was hurting her still. *I'm here for you now, Catherine. But you have to let me in.*

Later that evening, Logan announces that he's taking them both out for a birthday celebration meal. But first he gives Caroline a gift, beautifully wrapped in gold paper and gold ribbon. It reminds Catherine of Arthurs retirement present, so much has happened since then.

Caroline blushes gracefully, her cheeks pinking delicately. "Thank you, Logan, should I open it now?" she asks uncertainly.

He nods enthusiastically, and puts his arm around a stiff and silent Catherine.

Undoing the bow and peeling the paper off so as not to tear it, Caroline gasps when she lifts the lid of the box. Staring up at Logan, she thanks him, "I've never seen anything like it. It actually looks like me playing the piano..."

The lead crystal figurine is a delicate masterpiece, and Logan is thrilled that Caroline likes it. Smiling down at Catherine, he tips her face up for a chaste kiss. Knowing she would be embarrassed with anything more.

"You ladies had better get a move on, the table is booked for seven-thirty, and it's already six."

Caroline follows Mrs Baines to her room and thanks her for her help. "I don't mean to speak out of turn," Mrs Baines quietly closes the bedroom door, "but I feel there are some things that need to be said." She stops to gauge Caroline's reaction, and then continues when the young woman nods. "I've only known Catherine a few weeks myself, but I've become very fond of her and wouldn't want to see her get hurt. She really has had enough of that in her young life." Mrs Baines flushes awkwardly. "I just wanted to say, that's all."

"Thank you, Mrs Baines," Caroline smiles her sincere gratitude. "I need all the help I can get with Catherine. I thought I was frightened of the unknown, but she appears positively terrified. I really am beginning to wonder if I shouldn't move out in to a hotel after all. I'm sure my room won't have been taken yet."

"That's up to you, of course," Mrs Baines tells Caroline. "But I'd give it a few days and see how it goes. You'll have more opportunity to get to know each other here."

"Thank you, Mrs Baines; I'll give it a few days." Caroline sits on her bed, looking out of the window over the lovely grounds. Then she spots Catherine, wandering aimlessly on her own. "What are we going to do?" *I didn't think I'd feel like this, so protective and worried for a sister I didn't even know I had a week ago.*

The meal out is to be at one of the bigger hotels, and having been there before, Catherine knows she is expected to dress up. But she decides to wear one of her summer dresses, a mauve and pink affair that hangs in an A-line to mid-calf length beneath the fitted bodice.

What's the point, she's so much prettier. So alive. I'll look drab next to her no matter what I wear.

Logan is waiting downstairs in the hallway when Caroline emerges from her room and descends the staircase. In her full length copper coloured taffeta dress and her silky bob pulled back and secured at one side with a jewelled comb, Caroline looks amazing. Not knowing what to expect she had packed for all occasions, and is glad now that she had.

"You look lovely," Logan tells her then spots Catherine at the top of the stairs.

Shit. I knew it.

His smile widens as she comes down to join them. "Well, ladies, I shall be the envy of every man there when I walk in with the two of you. You both look stunning."

Arriving at the hotel, Logan passes the car keys off to valet parking then escorts the two women inside. They are shown through to a private room and a loud cry of "happy birthday" greets them immediately the doors are opened.

Both girls are stunned, then Caroline grins at Catherine, a mischievous look in her blue eyes. "Come on, sis', let's have some fun," and puts her arm through Catherine's and drags her in to the midst of the crowd of well-wishers.

Time and again people comment on their staggering likeness. Robert Kingsley makes a b-line for Caroline and herds her on to the dance floor. Again and again, he puts Caroline through her paces, she is his perfect match.

Despite her high heels, Caroline really lets her hair down. "Wow, you can really move." Robert is delighted and they move well together.

Her arms briefly wind around his neck. "You haven't seen my moves yet." Her smile is lascivious, and Robert responds instantly.

Spinning her out and away, he spins her back and this time his arms hold her to him. "So, you want to play."

You have no idea. Caroline is making her own rules now. She's had enough of men controlling her life and hurting her with their deceptions. "If...I decide to play, it will be on my terms," she tells him. *My terms! My game! My satisfaction!*

Robert is so taken aback he can't think straight. "Why don't we get a drink?" he asks when the dance ends. But as he walks off the dance floor Caroline continues to dance with Ben, who has seen his opportunity and acted fast.

"I like your moves," she laughs at Ben, and he pulls her into his arms for a close smooch. Their hips grind and their legs move in an erotic tangle that turns them in a slow circle. Her long dress hides their antics from the onlookers and the dance-floor is packed.

Ben can't believe his luck. Caroline actually seems to like him, and she is so much fun. Far more chilled out than Catherine.

As the dance ends, Robert steps up to re-take his place as Caroline's dance partner. Ben, however, has other ideas. From the side-lines Logan and Catherine are watching the men square up to each other and Logan passes his drink to Catherine. "Back in a minute."

"Caroline, I believe this dance is mine," Logan announces and sweeps her into his arms and away from the two men who are now staring after them in disbelief. "You are a very gregarious young woman," he tells her, but it does not sound like a compliment.

"Are you telling me off, Logan?" Her face tips up to his, cocked to one side observing and assessing her sister's future husband. "I'm a big girl, I can handle myself," Caroline tells Logan, and doesn't sound pleased at his censure. *I've had enough of men thinking I'll dance to their tune. I intend to start making my own sweet music. So get out of my way.*

"But can they," he smiles to lighten his words and swings her around to stem the conversation. Giving a small nod of his head at the end of the music, Logan offers his arm to Caroline and guides her back to where Catherine is waiting, still holding his drink.

Giving her a dazzling smile he bends to kiss her at the same time as relieving her of his drink. "Thank you, my darling. Disaster averted, I think."

"Don't be so sure," and she points with her chin at the two men shouldering each other as they make their way over to Caroline.

"Robert, Ben, may I get you both a drink," Logan asks politely, but when both men make to refuse his polite manner abruptly changes. "Gentlemen, just remember that is what you are and go take a walk outside if that's what it takes to cool off."

His tone brooks no argument and both men move off in opposite directions, both frowning their displeasure.

"That was a little high handed, don't you think." Caroline is clearly not pleased at Logan's interference, though the situation had become fraught.

Catherine gasps audibly, shocked at her sister's behaviour.

"Oh, don't worry, little sis'," Caroline smirks unattractively, "I'm not a bad girl, not usually anyway." *But I'm learning fast. Maybe bad girls have more fun. Not something I've had much of lately.*

"How do you know I'm the younger one?" Catherine asks a little miffed.

Caroline gives a delightful little giggle. "I don't, but for all intents and purposes, you are." When Catherine frowns, Caroline takes her glass out of her hands and leaves Logan holding the drinks. "Come on, sis' let's go."

Catherine doesn't get the chance to argue, and looks apologetically over her shoulder at Logan. But he just smiles his encouragement.

The music has changed to modern pop and in spite of her long gown, Caroline really gets some moves going. "Come on Catherine, this is fun," she laughs.

Catherine has only ever felt comfortable dancing with a talented partner who guides her through the moves — she isn't used to making up her own. Watching Caroline gyrate to the beat, and listening carefully to the music, Catherine starts to move with it.

"Hey, you're good," Caroline smiles widely, "just get a little looser and you'll be spot on." *Maybe Logan doesn't like her to let her hair down. Mmm. We'll have to do something about that.*

Catherine beams at her sister's praise, and realises she is actually having a good time. *Having a sister might not be so bad. Maybe.*

Getting up the next morning was not so much fun. Caroline moaned and covered her eyes when Mrs Baines pulled the curtains back. The sun is shining particularly brightly; Caroline frowns as Mrs Baines stands with a breakfast tray at the side of her bed.

"Mr Sayers thought you might appreciate a light breakfast in bed," Mrs Baines says kindly. "I've put a couple of Aspirin on the tray just in case you needed them." She is trying to hide her smile, but can't stop the corners of her mouth from twitching.

"Hmm," Caroline eyes the housekeeper suspiciously, but decides she really likes this straight talking motherly woman. "Well, Mrs Baines, I'm grateful to you. My head is definitely suffering."

"Just come down when you're ready," Mrs Baines gives a sympathetic smile, "Catherine is suffering too. I just took her a breakfast tray in, and a couple of Aspirin."

When they meet up an hour later in the sitting room, both girls look a little delicate and offer the other a tentative smile.

"How's the head?" Caroline asks Catherine, who holds a flat hand out and wavers it in a 'so-so' gesture that makes her smile. "Me too, I haven't let loose like that in a long time."

Catherine is surprised, and so is Logan, who is watching the two women interact with interest. "But, you seemed so...so..." Catherine shrugs her shoulders, not able to find the words to describe her sister's outgoingness.

"Hmm, I can see why you'd think that," and Caroline grimaces when flopping down in a chair jolts her head. "But really, I rarely get the chance to dance or go drinking – perhaps that's why The Numbskulls are hammering so loudly in my head this morning." Raising a hand to her temple, she presses a particularly sore spot.

"Oh, you too," Catherine beams at her frowning sister. "I used to love the Beano. The Numbskulls were my favourite characters. I loved the idea of all those little people doing who knows what to keep my bodily functions in check."

Caroline laughs cautiously. "Well, I think they are making their displeasure known. I swear they hid the Aspirin, or perhaps I just gave myself a doozy of a hangover," she smiles over at Catherine and turns to include Logan.

"Personally, my favourite was Denis the Menace," he grins mischievously. "Desperate Dan was pretty funny too," he adds, delighting in the easy atmosphere that is developing. And is even more delighted by Catherine's reactions to her sister.

Rolling her eyes at Logan and looking at Caroline, Catherine shakes her head, "Rich kid," she states by way of explanation. "He obviously got the Dandy too."

Trying hard not to show her surprise, Caroline laughs off Catherine's telling remark. "Well, we had the better of the two," she grins. *Were you so poor?* Her heart aches; she'd had both comics too, but wouldn't dream of letting on.

"What are your plans for today, ladies?" Logan looks from one to the other and smiles ruefully. "Hmm, not fit for much, either of you. Why don't you get some fresh air in the garden, it might help clear your heads."

"Actually, that sounds like a good idea," Caroline gets slowly to her feet. "Come on, let's show The Numbskulls we can act responsibly then maybe they'll take pity on us and stop with the hammering."

Catherine gives a shy giggle; she's still not sure about being on her own with her new sister. "Ok."

The garden is spectacular, bathed as it is in the bright sunshine that lifts the morning temperature to a comfortably warm 20 degrees C.

Both women are silent, at first. Then a pheasant plops down heavily on the lawn in front of them, making them both jump then giggle helplessly.

Tears of mirth are pooling in their eyes. "Fuck me!" Caroline gasps between giggles. "Do birds fall out of the sky often around here?"

But Catherine is laughing too hard to answer and just shakes her head for an answer.

"Well, that's good to know," and Caroline clasps a hand over her racing heart. "I don't fancy dying of a heart attack just yet – I have a lot of living to catch up on." *A lot of living to catch up on. And I will.*

Catherine's laughter finally subsides and she looks at her twin with curious eyes. "Why do you say that?" she asks tentatively. Warily.

Continuing to walk in silence, Catherine begins to regret asking the personal question.

"I recently found out that the man I thought I would marry has been cheating on me every time I was off on tour." It was not said with anger, but an edge of bitterness couldn't be hidden.

A gasp escapes Catherine before she can stop it. "Oh, god, I'm so sorry." And she realises that she means it.

"It's ok," Caroline lies easily, even to herself, "I'm over it. But I don't intend to let it happen again," she smiles ruefully over at Catherine. "I intend to take control of my own life, from now on. I'm sick of men having the upper hand. Even dad couldn't play it straight with me." *I trusted you. You're my dad - my hero.*

They come across a bench that Catherine has never found before. Both sit and enjoy the spectacular view. "He didn't tell you anything. From before, I mean," Catherine clarifies.

Shaking her head, Caroline looks very sad. "The first I knew of any of this was when Logan's letter arrived." Gathering her thoughts, she sits silently contemplating the recent past. Eventually she turns to regard her twin. "You know, I was so full of anger and resentment at first. Angry that dad had lied to me by omission for so many years – yet I'd given him plenty of opportunities to come clean when I asked him about mum. But he never told me anything; couldn't even bring himself to say her name." Again she falls in to a contemplative silence.

"And the resentment...?" *Is that directed at me?*

"You got to live with the mother I had always wanted," Caroline states simply, no trace of the old resentment. Turning towards Catherine, Caroline takes her sister's hand. "I'm so sorry that I wasn't there for you when mum died. I can't imagine what you went through."

Looking down at their joined hands, Catherine forces herself not to pull away as her instincts demand. "Do you know how she died?" At Caroline's silent shake of her head, Catherine sighs heavily. "It wasn't pretty, and it wasn't quick. She was raped, tortured and murdered." When Caroline gives a pained sob, she gives her sisters hand a supportive squeeze. "I'm sorry; I'm not good with tact and wrapping things up in a pretty bow." *Because it wasn't pretty. It was the worst of the worst, and you need to know that.*

Tears slide silently down Caroline's pale cheeks. "How old were you?"

"Almost ten." She turns away to look back at the house, trying to think of Logan, of Mrs Baines, of anything but the nightmare that she doesn't want to relive.

"It's ok," and Caroline returns the reassuring squeeze, glad that her sister hasn't pulled away from her. "I just want to know what happened to you. I heard you lived in foster care after mum died – what was that like?"

So, she doesn't know about the psychiatric centre. "As bad as it sounds, I suppose. I didn't have much, but it didn't seem to matter. None of the kids did." She shrugs it off. "But I missed my books," Catherine remembers, surprising herself. "I don't know what happened to them – one day they were there and then they weren't." She frowns. Why hadn't she remembered that before?

"Books...?"

Catherine turns back to look at her sister. Her identical twin. "Did anyone ever tell you that you had a 'gift'?" She mimes quotation marks in the air with her fingers. When her sister nods, Catherine continues with a resentful smile. "Yes, well, that's what they told me and my mum I had. A great and almighty gift of exceptional intelligence and ability. I have a photographic memory, and I'm a whiz with computers and programming," she states dully. "But I wouldn't call it a gift." *Not when your photographic memory keeps showing you snapshots of your mums terror and pain. I love you, mum.*

"I was three when I started playing along with the classical music dad likes to listen to. I had a toy grand piano and actually managed to play a decent tune on it," she laughs at the thought. "Dad was so impressed he got me piano lessons and by four I was playing in front of an audience." Her smile turns into a frown and Catherine finds herself listening more attentively. "I was hailed as a 'piano protégé', and I enjoyed the attention. I gather things were not so easy for you." *It doesn't sound like anything was. I'm sorry.*

"I was a pain. Always getting in to trouble," she admits with a self-deprecating grin. "I got bored easily, and I took it out on everyone else. Including mum," Catherine frowns, troubled by the memory. "That's why she worked all hours. I think she needed the break from me as much as she needed the money to keep me in books. They were the only thing that occupied me. Trouble is, I got through them quickly, and our local library was too far away to get to on a regular basis without a car." *It was no picnic for mum. Sorry mum.*

Chapter Three

Next morning, Mrs Baines serves up cereals and toast, with a cooked breakfast option for Logan, and the girls if they want it.

"I think I'll go in to the office today," Catherine tells Logan then turns to Caroline, "if you don't mind, that is."

Raising a surprised eyebrow, Caroline shakes her head. "Not in the least, but I'd like to come with you – you know, see where all that brainpower gets to work out." Then she laughs when Catherine blushes and looks uncomfortable. "I was only joking – but I really would like to see where you work. Do you mind?"

Fuck it. "It's just a couple of cramped offices," she grimaces down at her half eaten cereal. "But that reminds me," Catherine looks hopefully across at Logan, "I was wondering if you might have time to help me find some bigger premises. Ben intends to expand the workforce, by two I think. So...at least three decent sized offices would be good." She blushes even deeper, feeling uncomfortable talking about business in front of Caroline, and not sure if she should have asked Logan to help her out. *Shit. Will he think I'm taking advantage of his connections? Oh, fuck it.*

Logan smiles at her obvious discomfort. "Catherine, I would be very pleased to help you find more suitable offices." His smile turns in to a grin when she smiles up at him through her lashes. "If memory serves, I believe I have at least a couple of options you might like to take a look at."

Catherine frowns, forgetting that Caroline is watching quietly in the background. "I expect you to see that I don't get ripped off," she tells him, wagging her spoon at him. "Not like those bloody clothes shops you take me to," and begins chomping on her cereal with gusto.

Logan restrains his laughter, knowing that Catherine won't appreciate it. "They were boutiques, and very exclusive with exceptional designs and quality." He looks over to Caroline, who is smiling at the intriguing conversation. "Catherine doesn't like parting with her hard earned cash. Buying anything for more than five pounds causes her physical pain."

"Damn right!" Not giving Caroline time to respond, Catherine glares at Logan angrily. "Clothes are just clothes, I don't need some stuck up bitch looking down her nose at me when she's raking in a fortune in fucking commission at my expense!" Breathing hard and blushing wildly, she pushes up from her seat. "Oh, fuck it!" Without looking at either of them, she runs from the room and up to her bedroom. Their bedroom. Hers and Logan's.

Mrs Baines comes to the conservatory door after Catherine has left and gives both Logan and Caroline a disapproving frown.

"Damn!" Logan hisses quietly. "I should have known better than to tease her like that. I'll just go up and see if she's ok." But before he can rise from his seat, Caroline put's a restraining hand on his arm.

"Let me," she smiles reassuringly and gets up gracefully to leave the room.

Knocking on Catherine's bedroom door, Caroline opens it a fraction then goes in hurriecly when she finds her sister crying buckets on the bed. "Don't cry," she stokes Catherine's hair with a gentle hand, "please don't cry. I can't bear to see you like this." Then realises that it hurts to see her sister so upset, more than she would have believed possible just a few short days ago. *I'm here now; I won't let anyone hurt you again. I promise.*

Stifling her sobs, Catherine turns to look at Caroline. "No one's ever stroked my hair like that before."

Poor baby. "I would have done it every night to help you sleep if we'd been allowed to stay together," Caroline smiles then frowns when Catherine's brows draw together. "What...?"

"I don't know..." she whispers, "...it's just...a memory...I think..." looking at Caroline she pulls herself into a sitting position on the bed, "...of someone, you, tickling my hair. We slept in the same room, I think, maybe even in the same bed, and you used to play with my hair to help me sleep." Shaking her head, Catherine squeezes her eyes closed and the memory fades to nothing.

"I don't think that can be right," Catherine laughs it off, "I've never remembered anything like that before. I was probably just imagining it."

Nodding, Caroline decides to let it go, not wanting to upset Catherine by pushing the point. *Interesting. With your photographic memory maybe you have hidden memories. How exciting.* "So, do I get to see where my baby sister works," she teases, lightening the mood.

Taking a deep, juddering breath, Catherine nods her agreement. "But there really is very little to see. The offices are cramped and... You know..." she raises her brows looking at Caroline, "...I don't even know if I still have an office. Ha! Imagine that, and I'm supposed to be the boss." *Crap!*

Dressed in her favourite yellow sundress, Catherine pulls into the car park at the back of Compusafe. "That's Ben's car," she informs Caroline as they walk towards the office door, "I think he's in love with it."

"Not quite as sparkling as yours," Caroline turns back and smiles appreciatively at the two cars.

Catherine blushes wildly. "That's because mine is brand new. A birthday present from Logan," she continues when Caroline raises a questioning brow.

"I'd say wow, but that just doesn't seem to cover it." They turn and smile at each other, then burst in to a fit of giggles that continues even when they enter the outer office door.

"Catherine, you sound happy...Oh, and Caroline too, I didn't realise you were coming in, Catherine," Ben turns back to his boss but can't help his gaze flicking back to look admiringly at Caroline. She is dressed in a simple but short fitted sundress in bright fuchsia.

"I came for an update, and Caroline wanted to see where I work," she says, flicking a hand in Caroline's direction and making for her office.

"So, you're out exploring," Ben tries not to make an idiot of himself by talking about the weather. Then does it anyway. "Nice day for it," he smiles nervously; then winces when Catherine's voice bellows from her office. "Oh, crikey!" *Shit!*

"What the fuck has been going on?" Catherine is standing with her hands on her hips and her eyes blazing. "Ben! Get your arse in here!"

"Catherine, I don't appreciate..."

"I don't give a rat's arse what you do or don't appreciate," she glares at Ben as he comes to her open door, "but I don't appreciate coming in to my office to find it wrecked! Where the fuck are all my files?"

Caroline is way impressed to see that her sister has a backbone and is capable of using it to stand up for herself. *But perhaps this is not the best time for a visit.* "You know...," Caroline speaks up tentatively as she moves to Ben's side in the doorway, "...I can see that you're busy, and I don't want to get in the way. So, I'm just going to nip off and do a bit of shopping. My favourite pastime," she smiles at Ben, and then notices that her sister looks dumbfounded. "It can be very therapeutic," she informs Catherine with a smile, and then laughs when Catherine just grimaces. "I've got your mobile number, and you've got mine, so if I get lost or you have any problems, we can keep in touch."

Catherine eyes her sister uncertainly, feeling guilty at the thought of leaving her to fend for herself in a strange town. Not that Sheriton is big enough to get seriously lost in, she consoles herself. But still. "Are you sure? I don't think I'm supposed to leave you to your own devices – I'm sure Logan would have something to say about etiquette, or some such happy shit." She frowns down at her feet feeling awkward and gauche.

"I'm a big girl," Caroline smiles at Catherine; turning to Ben her smile becomes seductive. With a deft movement, out of sight of Catherine, she pushes a scrap of paper in to Ben's pocket. "I'll see you later. Don't work too hard," she calls over her shoulder and walks out of the front door and in to a gloriously sunny day.

Taking a restorative lung full of the wonderfully clean air, Caroline hitches her shoulder-bag up and begins her exploration of Sheriton.

It doesn't take long to reach the outskirts of the town centre. And here she spots a car hire company. *Well, I'm likely to be here for a few weeks, and I would like to explore some of the surrounding country side... Why not!*

The door has a bell that chimes as she opens it and walks in. Spotting a young man behind a desk she walks over, and is about to voice her enquiry when he looks up and chokes on the coffee he's just taken a sip of.

He coughs and splutters, turning puce — either with embarrassment or because he can't breathe, Caroline isn't sure which. "Is there somewhere I can get you a glass of water?" she asks, concerned.

But he holds his hand up to ask her to give him a minute, and eventually regains some control. "Can I...," his voice squeaks, he clears his throat and tries again. "Can I help you, madam?" He reaches for a tissue and tries to dab the smattering of coffee off his tie while distracting her with a beaming smile.

"If you're sure you're alright...?" And when he nods and smiles Caroline is reassured. "Well, I'll be in the area for at least a week, though hopefully longer, and I need a car."

Car keys in her bag, Caroline continues to walk in to the town centre as she's decided to pick the rental car up later. *What a delightful little town this is. Like an oldie-worldie film set.* Looking directly across the town square, she spots the Library and decides to pay a visit.

On the outside it looks like a very old schoolhouse. And on the inside she finds that it is, a very sympathetically converted schoolhouse that now has thousands of books lining its many shelves.

Walking over to the main desk, Caroline is greeted by an attractive woman with a welcoming smile. But as she draws nearer the smile falters and the woman's cheeks pale. "Caroline...?" The woman shakes her head as if to clear it. "Can I help you?" she asks, and tries but fails to restore her welcoming smile.

Caroline frowns silently, not sure if she'd heard the woman use her name or not. It had been spoken in such a breathy whisper. "I was wondering if you had microfiche copies of old newspaper articles?"

The Librarian smiles and steps out from behind her desk. "Of course, just over here." Caroline follows the neatly dressed woman with her light brown hair just as neatly pinned up in a bun. "There you are," and she waves a hand towards the microfiche reader. "If you would like to tell me which newspaper and the year you want to look at, I'll get it for you."

"I'd like the Sheriton Daily," Caroline specifies, then adds, "if you could go back sixteen years, and fifteen years that would be really helpful."

The woman frowns and her cheeks lose what little colour they had regained. Nodding she says, "I see...I see...I'll just get them for you."

Three hours later, Caroline has finished reading and is still drying her sore eyes. She's been crying almost the whole time – reading her mother's murder story in the newspapers has been a horrific revelation.

Did dad know about this? She hands the microfiche in at the Librarian's desk, and barely hears the woman ask her if she is all right. The sun is blinding and hot after the cool dim library.

Walking in a daze, back to the car rental office, Caroline comes to a difficult decision. After picking the red Corsa up, she drives hurriedly back to Logan's house. Arriving without getting lost, she is thankful that her mobile has a sat-nav app on it.

"I've decided to stay in a hotel, after all," Caroline tells Mrs Baines when she opens the front door. "I think that would be best," she sniffs, trying not to let the threatening tears fall.

Mrs Baines is wide-eyed and worried. "This isn't because of what I said..." But Caroline shakes her head emphatically.

"No. No. Not at all. I just want...I just need..." Mrs Baines pulls her in to a motherly embrace, rubbing Caroline's back as the tears come thick and fast. When her sobs grow less convulsive and her tears slow to a steady trickle, Mrs Baines guides Caroline in to the sitting room and on to a settee.

"Is this to do with Catherine or your mother?" she asks tentatively.

"Both," Caroline answers on a sob. "I never knew. I didn't realise what Catherine has been through – and all on her own," she sobs again, her sodden tissue doing little to dry her tears or her nose.

"Here," holding a box of tissues towards Caroline, Mrs Baines sighs deeply. "I remember when it all happened. The newspapers were full of it. We had reporters and TV vans all over the place. It was bedlam for a while." Her eyes go distant with remembering. "Of course, none of us knew then that Catherine had seen it all. Had been bound and gagged and forced to watch her poor mum die in the most horrific way." When she hears Caroline's startled gasp, Mrs Baines realises her mistake.

"I'm so sorry," she shuffles nearer to Caroline on the settee and takes her hand. "I thought, when you said about what Catherine had been through, that you knew all about it." *Talk about putting your foot in it! Lord help me!*

Caroline dries her tears and blows her nose. Then she stands up, determined to get her things together and move in to a hotel before Catherine or Logan come home. "Don't worry about it, Mrs Baines. I'd rather hear it from you than some village gossip."

Getting to her feet, Mrs Baines shakes her head. "It isn't common knowledge. From what Catherine was able to tell me, I gather all those involved were sworn to secrecy and a gag order imposed. She was a minor, and in a dangerous position." She looks up at Caroline's tear streaked face. "He was still out there, you see. And Catherine had seen him."

Rubbing her hands over her face, Caroline tried to gather her thoughts. "I need some time and space to take all this in, and I won't get that here."

Mrs Baines nods in agreement. "And you need to grieve," she told a surprised Caroline. "You've found your sister but your mother is beyond your reach. All those lost years that you can never get back, you need to allow yourself to admit the loss and acknowledge your feelings. Only then will you begin to move forward, and begin to forge a lasting bond with your sister."

When Caroline walks in to the lobby of the Lovett Hotel, she is holding one suitcase and pulling the larger one along on its wheels.

The receptionist welcomes her with a warm smile. "I telephoned about an hour ago – my name is Caroline Thornton."

"Yes, Ms Thornton, I took your call," the young woman stated pleasantly. "I reserved suite 211; it has a lounge and wonderful views over the surrounding country side." Holding a hand up to signal a waiting bellboy, the receptionist asks Caroline to sign in and hands her a key card.

"If you need room service, or to speak to myself or a colleague on reception, just press '0' on the telephone in your room. And to get an outside line, just press '9' before entering the number you want to call." Handing over a welcome pack, she continues, "It's all in here – welcome to the Lovett Hotel, if there's anything we can do to make your stay more enjoyable, please just ask."

Hmm, and how much is all this smiling civility going to cost me in tips!

The bellboy picks up her cases and takes them over to the lift. Following closely behind, Caroline takes the time to glance around at her surroundings. The building is very old, as are many of the buildings in Sheriton, and the decor is sympathetic to the era without being dark or oppressive. Beautiful.

Suite 211 is on the second floor. Caroline steps ahead of the bellboy, Martin she observes from his lapel badge, and uses the key card to open the door. Moving in to the room ahead of him, she holds the door open.

Setting the cases down in the bedroom, Martin returns to the sitting room and smiles shyly. "Is there anything I can do for you before I leave," he asks.

"No, Martin, but thank you for your help." Caroline makes to give him a tip but he smiles and shakes his head.

"The Lovett doesn't allow its staff to accept gratuities," he informs her. "They have a strict policy; it's to ensure the customer is satisfied with the service they receive – if they are, there's an opportunity to add a gratuity to the final bill. If not, we just ask that you inform the management of any complaints or dissatisfaction so that it can be addressed."

How refreshing.

Before Caroline can form a reply, her mobile rings and the bellboy leaves discretely.

Looking at the caller ID she doesn't recognise the number. "Hello." A delighted smile spreads across her face. "Ben, that was quick. Is Catherine still at work with you?" Chuckling to herself, Caroline can imagine Catherine blowing through the offices like a mini tornado, which is how Ben describes her behaviour since she left. "Well, I have to agree, she has an awesome temper – I never imagined." Sitting in a seat by the large window, Caroline is pleased when Ben asks her out.

"I'm not at Logan's anymore," she informs him. "No...there wasn't a problem. I just need my own space and privacy." Nodding she agrees to his suggestion of picking her up after work. "That sounds great, I'm staying at the Lovett Hotel...yes, it is lovely," she agrees. "Ok, that's fine. Just don't mention to Catherine that I've moved out, Mrs Baines is going to explain it to her so she doesn't get upset." *Well, that's the plan anyway.*

While she has her mobile out, Caroline decides it might be a good time to call her dad. After all, the only communication she's had with him is a couple of text messages. The first to tell him she had landed safely and the second to say that she'd arrived at Catherine's ok. *Here goes.*

"Hi, dad," she is glad that he sounds really pleased to hear from her. "Everything's great, dad, no worries. Catherine's fine, we were both a bit shocked at first, with us being identical and all, but on the whole we're getting on great." Caroline listens as her father talks about future performances and various contracts that need looking at when she gets back. "Ok, but don't book anything for the next two months, I think it's going to take at least that long for Catherine and I to get our heads around all this."

Her dad is surprised at the length of time Caroline expects to be away and is worried about how she will keep up her piano practice. "I'm staying at the Lovett Hotel now, dad. I just needed a little space and privacy – hey, maybe they have a piano here I could practice on, I'll ask and see. If not, I'll sort something out, don't worry." Laughing, Caroline listens to the catch up news her dad is bringing her up to date on. "Ok, dad, I'll call again in a couple of days, you take care, bye."

Heaving a heavy sigh of relief, Caroline feels a little guilty that she had been dreading calling her dad. But herself, her dad and Catherine have all been thrown off balance emotionally since this family reunion business started.

Not that she has any regrets. It has been scary at times, but she's also excited about a future with her twin sister in it.

That evening, when Ben comes to the hotel to pick Caroline up for their date, he is directed to the large lounge instead of to her room. Frowning, wondering if she had wanted an early drink, he makes his way through the lobby and off to the right to the lounge.

His eyes go wide when he walks in to the large room and sees that Caroline is playing the piano. Moving over to the long bar situated along the back wall, he takes a seat to listen. When he looks around he can see various staff members standing mesmerized by Caroline's playing.

Her hands are flying over the keys and the music she is creating is so beautiful and haunting. He tries to think if he's heard it before, but decides it must either be new or obscure.

The staff break in to spontaneous applause at the end, and Ben joins them enthusiastically. "Bravo," he grins broadly at Caroline when she turns and sees him walking towards her. "That was amazing. Truly amazing!"

Good timing, first date impressions are always tricky. "Thank you, kind sir," and she does a dramatic curtsy and laughs when he pulls her towards him for a hug.

"I Knew you played, of course," he smiles down at her as he holds Caroline at arm's length admiringly, "but I never dreamed you were so talented, you have a very rare gift." His eyes are bright and his smile wide as he turns and guides her towards the bar. "What would you like to drink?"

"Mmm...well...I suppose that depends on where we have it." Caroline smiles sexily. "How are you at casual friendships, Ben?"

He stops dead, not sure if he's misreading her signals, but Caroline is being so blatantly provocative. "I can do casual," Ben smiles and frowns not knowing what to expect next.

"Then let's go up to my suite and order room service. I'm hungry," she grins suggestively. *And you are definitely on the menu.*

Getting in the lift, Ben stands hesitant next to Caroline as they ride up to the second floor in silence. Taking out her key card she inserts it in the lock and shows Ben in to the suite. *Now then. Let's get down to it!*

Putting her shoulder-bag and key card down on the small coffee table, Caroline turns to Ben and all but devours him with a single look.

No, no, I don't think I'm reading the signals wrong. How lucky can a guy get?

"So, you can do casual, heh?" Her arms circle around Ben's neck and she pulls his head down for a mind-spinning kiss. *Wow! I can do anything, and I don't have to answer to anyone.* Pulling apart, they both look hungry and neither of them is thinking of food.

"Bedroom...?" Caroline asks, her eyes sparkling with laughter.

"Bedroom," Ben agrees with a low rumbling chuckle.

A trail of clothing lies in their wake, by the time they reach the bedroom only their underwear remains. *Nice body, Ben, now show me you can use it.* Their mouths gasp, their tongues vie for supremacy and their hands explore feverishly.

"Caroline, if you don't stop you'll cut this lovely tryst a lot shorter than I'm sure either of us would like it to be." He groans as she gives the hard length of him a firm squeeze before removing her hand from the inside of his boxers.

"Mmm...," she smiles salaciously, "...I'm up for a protracted sex session; I need to let off some steam." Then she lets out a giggling scream as Ben nips her shoulders and continues to feast on her slowly and deliciously.

Kneeling in front of Caroline, Ben massages her ankles and works his way up her very fine legs. His fingers massage her skin and his tongue tastes and teases. By the time he nears her lacy briefs, Caroline is panting with need and anticipation. *Holy Shit...aahh.*

"You taste good," he smiles up at her and while their eyes are still connected, moves forward to nibble on her clitoris.

As her knees buckle, Ben gives her a directed push so that she lands on the bed her feet still touching the floor. "Now you can lie back and enjoy," his thumb has replaces his teeth on her love bead and his fingers have found their way under her panties. "You are so hot and wet." He pulls her briefs to one side and plunges a single long finger in to her feminine heat.

Feeling her body coming to the boil, Caroline allows the feeling to wash over her and finds the release she needs.

Feeling her tighten and release, Ben removes his finger and replaces it with his tongue to taste her. Her scream of pleasure is music to his ears and he plays Caroline as expertly as she plays her piano. Plunging and nipping, licking and sucking, he sends Caroline over for a second time

"So lovely," he croons moving up her body. Nipping her earlobe he causes her to gasp when his lips and tongue explore. "Lie down," Ben whispers, and guides her to lie fully on the bed this time. But when he moves to continue his exploration of her lush body, Caroline decides to take control.

"Lie down, yourself," she laughs and rolls him off her and on to his back, taking him by surprise. "Now, let's see what we have here," and her hand moves down to find him, hard and ready for some action. "You can't have all the fun," she smiles sexily as her hand moves slowly up and down the length of him, anticipating what's to come. *I can't believe I'm doing this.* Then, not taking her eyes off his, Caroline lowers her head to kiss the tip of his manhood, and then her lips just barely take him inside her mouth. Watching his eyes close and his hips strain up with invitation, Caroline withdraws teasingly.

"Eager beaver," she giggles, then takes him completely off guard when she plunges forward, taking the full length of him right to the back of her throat.

"Fuck! Fuck!" Ben arches his back off the bed as the sensations that Caroline is inflicting course through his loins and ripple out through his entire body. "Shit," he cries out again when her teeth and tongue join in to pleasure him. Her mouth works him hard and Ben groans loudly with the effort of holding himself back. "Fuck me!"

Caroline laughs, feeling in control and liberated by her daring. "No, darling, I was hoping you would fuck me."

Ben doesn't need any encouragement; he flips her on to her back and plunges in hard. Her scream of pleasure only fires him on and he continues to hammer in to her until her breathing changes and he feels her body tightening beneath him. Leaning on his elbows, Ben's hands find her breasts and tug hard on her nipples surprising Caroline, and with a last hard push, catapults them both over the edge to a blissful release.

They don't speak for some time. When their breathing and heart rates finally return to somewhere near normal, Caroline leans up on her elbow to observe her new lover. *Finally, I'm in control and can do as I please. Who cares if it's just a one off, at least this way my heart doesn't get broken.*

"Are you still alive in there?" Caroline strokes Ben's floppy hair back from his eyes, and when they open she grins down at him then bends to kiss him gently, lazily, enjoying the afterglow of extremely good sex.

Chapter Four

"How about a nice refreshing shower?" Caroline asks when Ben finally stops kissing her. Her eyes have a glazed look about them, and Ben is fairly sure that the shower is second on Caroline's mind.

"Great idea," he chuckles wickedly, "then we can get clean at the same time as getting down and dirty."

Bliss, a man after my own heart.

Diving off the bed with a girlish giggle, Caroline manages to evade Ben's attempts to tickle her. "I didn't say you could shower with me," she protests playfully when he makes to get in the double shower with her, "but if you promise to scrub my back I'll let you in." Stepping back, she presses a button for the shower to start and bathes them both in wonderfully warm water.

"I'll scrub your back," Ben laughs, and putting shower gel on a sponge he circles his finger in the air to tell Caroline to turn around. "But I'll start up here first," and he circles the sponge slowly but firmly across her shoulders, concentrating on her nape after lifting her hair out of the way. His lips follow in the sponges wake, drawing a little moan from Caroline. Continuing to circle the sponge, he moves lower down her back until he reaches the base of her spine where he places a gentle kiss.

Jesus, this feels so great. Don't stop now.

Her buttocks are small and firm, and while he concentrates the sponge on one, his mouth concentrates on the other.

Please, this is exquisite torture.

When he swaps sides, Caroline moans loudly, partly in pleasure and partly in frustration.

I need more. I need much, much more!

But Ben is enjoying his explorations and carries on down her lovely long legs. He kisses the back of her knee then moves across to her other leg, only this time he works up from her ankle.

Leaning both hands against the wall, Caroline sighs when the sponge moves between her legs and Ben uses it to stimulate her in ways she's never dreamed of. "I want to taste every single inch of you," then he shocks her by pushing her legs apart before turning away from her to virtually lie on the floor of the shower and bringing his head face up between her legs.

Oh god!

When his tongue pushes in to her, Caroline struggles to stay standing as her knees begin to tremble. He is holding her hips, pulling her closer so that his tongue can plunge and tease deeper.

Holy fuck!

"Ben, you have to stop," she gasps, then flings her head back as his tongue finds nerve endings she didn't know she had. "Please, I can't breathe...I can't...I can't..." Her scream is loud and long as an orgasm rips through her, bringing her to her knees. But Ben doesn't stop; his tongue and his mouth continue to plunder, dragging her orgasm out to almost tortuous lengths.

Only when he feels her shudders quiet does he allow his head to fall back on to the shower floor and look up in to her dazed face. "Jesus, Ben," Caroline catches her breath then looks down at him and laughs. "If we don't get up you're going to drown, and I don't fancy telling the police how it happened."

"Oh, I don't know," Ben has to laugh at the thought, "I think they'd envy me such a sweet death."

Naked and laughing they get to their feet and eye each other greedily.

Ben's arousal is fully evident, and Caroline eyes him like she's contemplating a good meal. Reaching out her hand, her fingers circle him and move with slow deliberation. "I want this where your tongue has already been, but first..." Dropping to her knees under the flow of water, she tips her head back and allows her mouth to fill. Then she leans forward to take Ben in to her mouth, swirling the water around him with her tongue. When her mouth eventually empties of water, Caroline licks him like an iced lolly. *Mmm, lovely.*

Ben is straining against his instincts to push himself fully in to her mouth; this is Caroline's game and if she's trying to drive him crazy she's succeeding.

Her teeth literally nibble down and up the length of him then bite him gently but firmly as she takes him in to her mouth. She's fraying his nerves then shatters them completely when she sucks with all her might, gradually taking more and more of him in to her mouth. His groans are loud, long and Caroline loves to hear him.

"Caroline, stop...you're driving me over the edge."

But Caroline is more than happy to oblige and continues to work him thoroughly and purposefully. *Come on Ben, I want all of you.* Putting her arms around him she grabs his tight buttocks and pulls him to her, sucking fiercely.

"Oh, christ...," and Ben has no choice but to find his release in her wonderful, tortuous mouth. "Caroline, I don't know whether to apologise or thank you." He's still trying to get his breath and his heart is beating triple time. Helping Caroline to her feet they stand together under the warm cascade of water.

"I think we had better dry off before we start to wrinkle," she giggles light-heartedly, "not very attractive."

Holding a hand to her cheek, he dips his head to kiss her gently. "You could never look unattractive," he kisses her again, more thoroughly, "you are beautiful."

Stepping out of the shower, they dry each other off very thoroughly.

The towels fall to the floor and their nakedness is complete again. "Let's order room service," Caroline suggests with a lusty smile. "We need to keep our energy up after all."

A couple of missed calls on her mobile tell Caroline that Catherine tried to get in touch the night before. *Shit*.

"Hey, Catherine, are you ok?" Not knowing what to expect after moving out without telling her, she is surprised to hear Catherine sounding 'normal'.

"Sounds great," Caroline's smile is wide and bright, "we could get lunch here in the hotel or in town if you fancy." Then she frowns at Catherine's alternate suggestion. "At your place – you mean with you and Logan?" But no, and now she's even more confused. "I didn't realise you had a separate place, I suppose I just assumed you and Logan have been living together for a while."

Listening to Catherine's plans to pick her up at midday, Caroline feels nervous, apprehensive. "Ok, I'll be waiting in the hotel reception, see you later." Something is not right. Unless her usually good instincts are completely letting her down, Catherine is worried about something.

Telephoning reception, she asks if the lounge is free for her to practice on the piano. Getting the ok, Caroline picks up her shoulder-bag and her key-card and makes her way down to the lounge.

The grand piano is a lovingly cared for treasure and Caroline enjoys the feel of the old ivory. *Like an old friend, your tone is warm and welcoming.* Running her fingers over the keys, she plays a few exercise pieces then takes a deep breath and steadies herself.

When Caroline's fingers next touch the keyboard, the music she entices from it is enthralling. Another original piece, she loses herself in the music and the pleasure she gets from playing. It has always been like this. Even as a small child her love of the piano and the music her little fingers had been able to create on it, had driven her to practice and improve exponentially. The masters had raved over her, encouraging her dad to enroll her in The Royal College of Music.

Her life revolved around her music. Caroline's childhood was lost before she ever realised it was passing her by. But she had never been unhappy. Just isolated, as the only young people she came in to contact with could be very snide and spiteful, calling her a freak, and telling her that her talent was unnatural.

But when Caroline played, none of that mattered. Her world was her music, and it was all she had needed. Until she met Clive. *Fucker!*

The music changes with the hurtful memory. Her hands are flying, her eyes burning with unshed tears. *I loved you. Why wasn't I enough? Why!*

She plays non-stop for two hours. Is physically and emotionally exhausted which, in itself, is oddly satisfying. As if sensing her distress, the listening staff do not applaud this time, but make themselves scarce instead.

Caroline walks up to the bar and orders a tall glass of iced soda water. She misses her PA, Ellisa. More than just working for her, Ellisa is a good friend and confidant. She had been invaluable during the painful breakup with Clive. Ellisa had kept her sane, had helped her to keep her thoughts and feelings in check and to use her music to pull her through.

As long as she had her music she had life. Whether she had love was another matter. *I don't need it or want it now. I can be my own woman – I proved that with Ben last night. I don't need another Clive. From now on I decide who and when and how!*

"I thought you were going to wait for me in reception?" Catherine frowns as she walks in to the lounge, and the barman does a comical double take. "It's twelve-fifteen, did you forget me?" Feeling awkward, Catherine blushes and looks down at her feet.

"I most certainly did not," Caroline's face lights up at seeing her sister. "I just did what I always do, got lost in the music and lost track of the time. Do you want a drink before we go?" she offers.

But Catherine shakes her head and the two of them walk out arm in arm. "You know," Caroline smiles slyly, "we've missed out on years of fun. Just imagine what we could have gotten up to, no one can tell us apart except for my hair being longer."

Catherine has to laugh at Caroline's childish look of mischief. "Do you think that's why they split us up – do you think we were already a handful?"

There was hurt in her sister's voice, Caroline could hear it. "It doesn't matter why anymore. We've found each other and no one will ever separate us again." But Catherine doesn't look convinced and Caroline shakes her arm. "I mean it, sis, I lost you once I won't lose you again. Not for anything." *You're the missing part of me that I never knew was lost, and I'm yours. You are not alone now, Catherine, I'm always going to be here for you.*

Getting in to Catherine's car, they make their way to her old one room bedsit and Caroline gets the shock of her life.

"Christ almighty, sis, you live here...in just this one room?"

"I've lived here since I was seventeen," Catherine's chin goes up and her tone becomes defensive, "it's always been enough for me, and it was my first ever home of my own."

Caroline wants to cry. To think of her sister living all alone in this place is heart-breaking enough, but for her to think of this lonely place as home is devastating. "I'll buy you a house of your own, and I'll be able to stay with you between tours and concerts. We can take a look at properties this afternoon, and we can plan the decoration and furniture..." She tails off when Catherine firmly shakes her head.

"I have money, Caroline; I just don't care about having it." She looks at the bemused expression on her sister's face and knows she is thinking the same as everyone. "I've never had much, mum and I got by but there was never much left over for luxuries. I suppose I just got used to being happy with less." She shrugged her shoulders and moved over to fill the kettle and make a hot drink. "Coffee or tea?"

Plumping for coffee, Caroline takes a stroll around the room then settles in its only chair. "So, why no photos of mum?"

Not answering immediately, Catherine takes out two mugs and puts a teaspoon of coffee in each. "Do you take sugar?" *This is going to be hard.*

"No thanks." *I don't want to upset her, but we need to talk.*

Sitting cross-legged on her bed, Catherine tries to pull the courage together to face telling her sister exactly how their mum died. "I find it hard to look at mums photos and not see her looking back at me with terror and agony in her eyes." *Even without the photos, I see her suffering every night I close my eyes.*

Nodding, Caroline tries to understand. "It's no good my saying I know how you feel, or even that I understand, because I can't," she frowns and sighs, "I wasn't the one who had to suffer through it all with her."

Catherine isn't slow at picking up on the fact that Caroline seems to know more than she ought. "Who told you that I was there?" *And what else did they tell you – is that why you've been so nice? Pity.*

"Please don't be angry, it was an honest mistake," Caroline tries to defend Mrs Baines' slip-up. "I came back from the library in tears, I'd just read the newspaper articles about mum's death and told Mrs Baines that I couldn't believe what you'd had to go through all on your own." Cocking her head to one side, she purses her lip. "She assumed I meant the ordeal you'd suffered during the actual attack; please don't be too hard on her. She cares about you so much." *And so do I.*

"I know, though I have no idea why," Catherine smiles and shakes her head in wonder. "But I'm relieved to know that you have a lot of the background information. I wasn't looking forward to going in to all the grisly details." Frowning at the thought, she gets up off the bed as the kettle comes to the boil and finishes making the coffee.

Taking a mug over to Caroline, she has to pinch herself mentally to realise that all this is real. She has an identical twin sister, and she is here in her tiny bedsit having a cup of coffee. *Surreal.*

"Thanks." Waiting for Catherine to make herself comfortable on her bed, Caroline tries to organise her thoughts and questions. "It didn't make pleasant reading, but I forced myself to read all of the articles. I feel guilty for not being there for mum, and I feel even guiltier for not being there for you." Shaking her head, Caroline tries to reason things out in her mind. "And the worst thing I can't get my head around is why dad didn't bring you home to live with us after mum died." Her head and shoulders droop. Her dad has always been her hero, but in something as important as this, he's let her down badly. *Why, dad? Why would you leave your own daughter out there on her own, and after living through such a terrible nightmare?*

"I don't care that he left me here," Catherine's chin juts out defiantly. "I never knew him and never want to. He left mum alone and she struggled to make ends meet, never mind the fact that he wasn't there to protect her when she needed him." *At least she didn't suffer alone. I'm so sorry, mum.*

"But, didn't mum tell you why they split up?" Caroline's eyebrows draw together perplexed. "From what dad said he didn't have a choice. Mum decided that she wanted a divorce and nothing dad said would change her mind. He's never stopped loving her," Caroline protests on her dad's behalf. "And he's never so much as looked at another woman in all this time."

"That doesn't make sense," Catherine's breathing is becoming difficult and the pain in her stomach is getting suddenly worse. Wrapping her arms about her and rocking back and forth, Catherine tries and fails to assimilate this new information. "Mum didn't look at another man either. I always thought she was pining after a man that had walked out on her – on us. I didn't even know if they'd been married." *I don't understand, mum. You never even spoke his name, that's why I never asked about him – I thought you'd loved him and hated him for leaving us, so I did too.*

Seeing her sister's obvious distress, Caroline crosses the room to sit beside her on the bed and put a comforting arm around her shoulder. "I'm sorry I've upset you, but I think we both need to be as honest as we can to find out what really happened." Hugging Catherine to her, Caroline instinctively reaches up to stroke her hair and tickle it between her fingers. Feeling her sister relax in to her side, Caroline's heart is breaking for the years they have lost.

"I feel like sucking my thumb," Catherine chuckles softly. *I saw that, I didn't just think it.* "I think that was another memory. I can't remember ever sucking my thumb, but I think I used to when you tickled my hair, when we were little."

Giving her shoulders a squeeze, Caroline has to swallow sudden tears. "I wish I could share your memories. It would be wonderful to remember us actually together." Her hand renews its task of stroking and tickling Catherine's hair, and Caroline's thoughts turn to the woman in the library. "When I went to the library to find out about mum, I spoke to the librarian to ask for the microfiche records of the relevant newspaper articles and I swear she paled noticeably."

Sitting upright to look at Caroline, Catherine tries to think who she might mean. "Oh, that might have been Erin," Catherine smiles. "Erin Vandivier was mums best friend. She was devastated when mum died. She came to the funeral and I remember thinking how very upset and sad she was."

"I suppose it could have been the shock of seeing me looking so much like you but with longer hair," but Caroline's instincts tell her there is more to it. "The thing is...," she hesitates, not wanting to upset Catherine again, but needing to get to the truth, "...when I entered and she saw me for the first time, I could have sworn she used my name. Sort of, in shock from seeing someone she knew from the past."

"Hmm, well, I suppose that is possible," Catherine considers, raking up memories of her mum with Erin. "In fact, I remember mum saying that they had been friends since junior school. I think they would have done just about anything for each other."

Except take you in when you had no one else!

"If that's true, then perhaps mum confided in her about the divorce and why she was so determined about it. Really, Catherine," she reiterates solemnly, "Dad loved her – he told me before I came here that he has never stopped loving her and honestly doesn't know what he did wrong. Yet he's never suspected there was another man involved – I don't think he believed her capable of that kind of deceit."

Catherine's cheeks redden with sudden temper. "I should bloody well think not! Mum was an honest, hardworking, and loving person and I never saw her take up with anyone else. Ever!" *Then why, if he really loved you, why did you make him leave?*

"I think we should go speak to Ms Vandivier," Caroline suggests firmly. "She could hold the key to this whole bloody mess. And, I don't know about you, but I want to know why we were separated – and it better be bloody damn good!"

Catherine drives them both to the library and parks in the rear car park. To Caroline she looks nervous, and for the first time wonders if she should have done this on her own. *What if Catherine has her saintly illusions of mum smashed by some awful revelation?*

The library is almost empty. Looking around for Erin Vandivier, Catherine spots her with a trolley of books that she is re-shelving. "There she is," Catherine points in the librarian's direction and starts to make her way over. "Mrs Vandivier, do you mind if we have a word?"

Erin turns to see both twins heading her way and drops the small pile of books she is holding. "Of...of course," she mumbles, diving to pick up the fallen books.

Caroline decides to take the bull-by-the-horns. "You don't seem very surprised to see us together; did you know that Catherine had a twin? An identical twin," she emphasises.

Erin looks at Catherine. "Yes, I'm afraid I did. And I'm sorry if you think I did wrong in not telling you, Catherine, but your mum made me promise. She thought she was doing it for the best."

For the best! Fuck that!

Holding up a hand to stay her sister, Catherine suspects there is more than just the divorce and consequential separation of two little girls going on here. *You're hiding something, it's written all over you.*

"My mum is no longer here and, as you can see, my sister and I have found each other despite your best efforts." She notes the paling of the older woman's cheeks and just knows that her suspicions are right. "You were my mum's best friend for many years, she confided in you and no doubt you in her. So why did she insist on the divorce?" *Please, please, don't let it be over another man. Please.*

"Catherine, please...I'm at work and if I had anything to say this wouldn't be the time or place," Erin swallows nervously, looking around to see if they are being overheard. "Not that I have anything to say. Your mum was the best friend I ever had; I respected her privacy then and still do now. Perhaps you girls should do the same." Straightening her already straight cardigan, Erin puts a nervous hand up to tidy her already perfect hair. "Children don't always have the right to know everything about their parent's private life – that's all I'm saying." And with that she pushes her book trolley to the furthest end of the library and disappears from view.

"Well, that was a resounding failure," Caroline huffs as they step back out in to the warm sunny day. *But she knows something.*

"Not at all," Catherine disagrees with a look of determination that causes her sister's eyebrows to rise. "You forget, sis'" she smiles as she uses Caroline's familiar term and waggles her fingers in the air, "you might use these for getting a tune out of a piano – I use them for getting information out of a computer. And I'm damned good at it." Her blue eyes gleam fiercely. *I found your killer, mum, now I'm going to find out what happened to make you push dad out of our lives.*

"I'll have you know I do more than just get a tune out of a piano," Caroline bristles, "I make the piano sing to the audience. And yes," she straightens her shoulders and lifts her chin, "I'm damned good at it too!"

They looked at each other, both bristling but for very different reasons. "Did we just have our first fight?" Caroline's mouth softens in to a smile.

On cue, both girls burst in to fits of giggles until their eyes begin to stream. Caroline pulls Catherine in to a sisterly hug and Catherine hesitantly returns it.

"Come on sis', we're going to the hairdressers," Caroline announces, and Catherine just looks stunned at the complete non-sequitur.

"I should have known better," Ben berates himself for the thousandth time that morning. "I fall in love with one sister then I'm fool enough to get involved with the other." He looks at himself in the mirror over the sink in the tiny loo at their too small office premises. "It'll all end badly, my lad," and he shakes a stern finger at his reflection. *Oh, for fuck's sake. I'm going bloody mental!*

Returning to his office, Ben looks through the applicants for the two positions he's advertised. The work has been pouring in, and while he's been able to sort a few of the minor jobs himself he can't possibly hope to manage the bigger contracts. "And who knows when her majesty will deign to come back!"

"Ok, this one looks promising." He frowns when he reads the qualifications. *Hmm, got a slightly higher result in his compu-science degree. Fucker. Still, he won't know that!* "And you're not bad either." He sticks out his bottom lip and plucks at it while he reads, not hearing the office door go.

"That's a very bad sign," the visitor says from Ben's doorway, "talking to yourself is said to be the first sign of madness, you know."

"Fuck me!" Ben gasps then gapes, there are two identical Catherines now stood in his office. "What the hell...?"

"Oh, so you got around to advertising for someone to help out." Picking up one of the applications the other girl begins to read.

"But did you take a look at the Carver account?" the first one says, hands on hips in a stance Ben thinks he recognises.

"No, Catherine, I didn't," and Ben smiles thinking he's beaten them at their own game.

Then the other puts the application form down and mirrors the hands-on-hips stance of her sister. "Then I suggest you get straight on it after you've finished looking through this bunch of no-hopers." *Ha! This is great!*

Looking from one to the other, Ben gives up. "Ok, ok, you got me." He holds his hands up in surrender and grins. "But please, if you value my sanity at all, tell me that only one of you is ever going to be working here," and he shakes his head as if dazed, "I really don't think I could take working with two Catherines." *Shit! One is quite enough.*

"Bloody damned cheek!" Catherine flushes bright pink with indignation.

"Ha, gotcha," Ben shoots out a pointy finger at Catherine. "Just don't move and I'll know who's who!"

"We need practice," Caroline giggles and Catherine can't help but join in.

This could be really hilarious. I wonder if Logan could tell us apart?

"Ok, look," Catherine clears her throat and tries to use her business voice, "I'm going back to Logan's; he's lined up a couple of properties for me to look at." Then she tilts her head regarding Ben with an impish smile. "But I won't sign anything until you've had a look too – alright partner?"

"Fine, you go look..." Ben turns and stares, "...did you say partner?" *Holy fuck! I thought I'd missed the boat on that one.*

Grinning, Catherine nods enthusiastically. "I can't manage without you, Ben. Does a 60:40 split sound ok?"

Ben's mouth gapes and closes then gapes again.

"That's the best impersonation of a Guppy I've ever seen," Caroline laughs.

Ben seems to recover himself. "It's just, so unexpected." His grin widens from ear to ear. "Of course, if you really think a 60:40 split is fair, who am I to refuse a controlling interest?" *Partner! Holy fucking shit!*

"Funny guy," Catherine smiles and shakes her head, "so you're saying yes to the partnership?" When he nods and grins foolishly, Catherine grins too. *Thank christ for that.* She is so glad they are back to being best friends; it had gotten sticky there for a while, but it has all worked out. "I'll ask Logan to get his solicitor to draw up a formal contract. It shouldn't take long." Pointing with her chin at the applications, she asks, "How long do you think it will take you to employ someone – is there anyone interesting among them?"

"As a matter of fact, there are at least a couple," Ben tries to pull his grin in to a more suitable business-like expression but inside he's dancing a jig, the corners of his lips trembling and Catherine raises her eyes to the ceiling. "I'm going to contact the ones I'm interested in this afternoon and if they can make it for interview tomorrow, so much the better."

"Well, since you've already turned me out of my office, I shall continue to work from home. I mean Logan's," she corrects quickly, blushing when she notices Caroline's raised eyebrow. "So, they can sit on opposite sides of my desk, it's big enough as a temporary measure. Then we'll need to sort out new furniture for the new offices. I thought three would do, what do you think?"

Logan isn't home when the girls arrive, but Mrs Baines is. They manage to keep a straight face when she gapes at them, but Catherine takes pity on her. "Do you think Logan will tell us apart?" she asks Mrs Baines.

"I'd like to say, of course, but I'm not so sure." She shakes her bemused head. "You are so incredibly alike. And when did you buy the dresses?"

"Today," Caroline fills her in. "We came out of the library and I decided to get my hair cut just like Catherine's. But we couldn't leave it there – we went in to a boutique that Catherine knows and Selma got us sorted out." Both girls giggle. "You should have seen her face, it was a picture."

"I'm sure it was," Mrs Baines laughs with them. Then they all turn when the front door sounds and heralds Logan's return home. "Quick, in the conservatory," Mrs Baines hurries them away while she goes to distract Logan.

The two girls strike identical poses on the comfy seating near the back windows. Both try to keep straight faces when Logan walks in obviously taken by surprise. "Good grief," his shock is total but a sly smile tugs at the corner of his luscious lips. "I'd say you have me at a disadvantage, but..." he crosses the conservatory and pulls one of the girls to her feet, then proceeds to kiss her most thoroughly. "Mmm, I'd know my woman anywhere," and Catherine blushes down to her roots. *Bloody Nora! Thank god he knew who I was. Or, did he? Hmm!*

Hell's bells, that man can kiss! "Well, after watching that I almost wish you'd picked the wrong sister," Caroline laughs, then has to back-track when Catherine's face falls. "Just kidding, sis', I've got my own date," she grins and shifts to tucks her legs up beneath her.

Logan and Catherine both look stunned. "But, where did you ever meet someone so soon?" *You're so full of confidence. Perhaps that's how Logan knew, you shine with it.*

"You introduced us." Caroline smiles as her sister looks nonplussed and Logan looks like the penny has just dropped. "Ben, we had our first date last night." Oh boy, and what a first date that was. Phew!

"But...but...you can't...," she flounders, taken completely by surprise, "...not with Ben." *He's in love with me. Shit!*

"I assure you I can, and did," Caroline giggles. *And will again if I have my way.*

Watching Catherine's reaction, Logan finds the situation interesting. "Not jealous, are you Catherine?" He's smiling but Caroline can sense an undercurrent.

"Don't be an idiot." Catherine gives him a swift back hand in the stomach. "But I do think Caroline should know."

"Hmm, maybe." Logan isn't so sure. *Why put a spoke in the wheel if Ben is starting to move on – but then, maybe he's using Caroline as a substitute for Catherine. After all, you can barely tell them apart.*

"Spill, for heaven's sake!" Caroline is looking from one to the other in exasperation.

Catherine's cheeks go pink as she tries to find the right words.

"He's in love with Catherine." Logan beats her to the punch. "At least, that's what he told her not so long ago."

"And he's still alive?" Caroline smiles and raises her eyebrows at Logan.

"Ah, well, I won the girl so I had some sympathy for him," Logan takes a seat opposite the two women, Catherine having sat back down next to her sister. "Had I been in danger of losing Catherine, I might have had to beat him to a pulp," and he gives the same demonstration that Mrs Baines had given him and slams a clenched fist noisily in to his palm.

Catherine pales. "You wouldn't!" *But it's kinda sexy to think you might.*

Laughing at the two of them, Caroline can see the love between them. *I had what you have, once. Or, at least, I thought I did.* "Don't fret over me, sis'," she gives Catherine a gentle dig with her elbow, "I'm a big girl, I can take care of myself. Ben's just a bit of fun," then she gives a telling wink, "actually, more than a bit, if you get my meaning," and laughs when Catherine looks shocked.

"But, you've only just met him!" *Christ all bloody mighty!*

"And your point is?"

"My point is you'll end up getting hurt;" Catherine looks sincerely worried, "or Ben will." *And I don't want that for either of you.*

Shaking her head, Caroline laughs her sister's concerns off. "I've learned my lesson in that department. I have no intention of letting my heart get involved with anyone. Not for a very long time, anyway." *I'm in the driving seat this time, and I'm staying there!*

Catherine is surprised at how strongly she feels to think someone broke her sister's heart. *I don't know you, but on some level I remember and I love you.* "What happened?"

"If you'll excuse me, ladies," Logan gets up and makes to leave the girls to talk, "I'll just see about getting us all a drink – what would you like?"

Smiling her thanks for his tact, Catherine opts for coffee.

"I'd kill for a cup of strong tea, no sugar," Caroline smiles her thanks.

Once they are alone, Caroline takes a deep breath and explains all the gory details about Clive, and how she found out about Jenna and all his other sexploits. "I can hardly believe that I had no idea," she tells Catherine. "I mean, you hear that line all the time and I've always thought, no way, there have to be tells. But honestly, there weren't."

Sighing deeply, Caroline lets her guard down and Catherine can see the depth of her heartache. "When he was with me, except for that last time, Clive was the most attentive lover a woman could wish for. And talk about romantic – he would turn up on tour, completely out of the blue, with roses and champagne and we'd make love all night." Rubbing her hands briskly over her face, Caroline swallows back the threatening tears. *I loved you, you bastard!*

"Anyway," she smiles determinedly, "that's the past. From now on I'm going to have a good time and sod what people think!" *Fuck them all!*

If only Catherine could believe her sister is as tough as she makes out. "I'm sorry," she reaches out a hand and lays it over Caroline's, "that you were hurt, and that I wasn't there for you." *But I'm here now.*

Well that did it. Both girls hug and shed a few tears — they have the rest of their lives to get to know each other better, but the love is already there between them.

Chapter Five

"Now, this is what I call celebratory sex," Ben groans as Caroline moves back up the bed having pleasured him almost to the point of toppling him over the edge.

Giving a sexy laugh, Caroline moves over him, bends to give him a teasing kiss and takes him inside her.

"Mmm," she croons in to his mouth. Pushing back, Caroline moans with the exquisite fullness he gives her. Sitting up she begins to ride him, slowly at first then arching her back in response to the sparks of electricity coursing through every nerve in her body.

When Ben's hands cup her breasts and he flicks his thumbs over her nipples, Caroline can't help the loud groan that escapes her. "Christ, Ben." Cresting her first climax, she falls forward and takes his mouth hungrily.

Their tongues seem to have their own mating ritual and its Ben's turn to give a guttural groan.

Flipping Caroline on to her back, he pulls out of her and she gives a whimper at the loss. "Not for long, baby," and he moves down her body to thrust his tongue inside her as a temporary replacement. But what he could do with that tongue was amazing and Caroline had to grip the sheets to steady her world. "Let go, Caroline," and he moves to nibble on her clitoris while his fingers work her relentlessly, "fly for me," and moments later he gets the response he's after. As her orgasm begins to rack her body he moves over Caroline, thrusting in to her taking her even higher.

When she screams his name, Ben circles his hips and pushes her legs back to thrust even deeper. He can feel her tightening around him and follows her with his own explosive release. "Jesus, Caroline," he collapses over her, then shifts his weight to one side, "we'll kill each other at this rate."

But they are both wearing extremely satisfied smiles, and nothing else.

His hand strokes gently up and down her arm and his eyes are studying her contented expression. "Making love with you is like nothing I've ever experienced," he murmurs softy, moving his hand up to caress her cheek.

But her response is not what he expects at all. "Is that what we're doing, Ben? I thought you said you could do casual." It wasn't a question, it was a warning and he knew it.

"Does that mean I'm not allowed to care, Caroline?" Leaning up on one elbow, Ben looks questioningly in to the blue depths of her wary eyes.

With a humourless laugh, Caroline springs out of bed before Ben can stop her. "You're in love with Catherine – I get it. I'm a good substitute, and I get that too. Now, I'm going to take a shower, you can join me or not, it's up to you."

With a shrug of her slender shoulders, Caroline turns to enter the bathroom, and Ben is left thunderstruck on the bed.

When she steps under the wonderfully warm refreshing shower, Caroline can't help regretting her outburst. It isn't Ben's fault she is damaged goods, and maybe he does care in a superficial casual sex way. And that was all she wanted, wasn't it*? I don't think I'll ever be able to love again – I don't think I dare.*

Emerging from the shower with a bath sheet wrapped around her, Caroline is surprised to see Ben already dressed and sitting on the edge of the bed. "I'm going to head off," he tries to smile and sound casual, but fails spectacularly.

Crossing the room, Caroline lays a hand on his pale cheek. "Ben, I didn't mean to hurt you – I just think it's better to be honest and up front." Placing a gentle kiss on his forehead, she moves to sit beside him on the bed. "I asked for a casual friendship because my heart is hurting too. So, maybe we can help each other to mend, even just a little."

He reaches over to take her hand in his. "You are not a substitute for anyone, and yes I'm hurt that you would think I'd use you that way." Shaking his head in disbelief, Ben tries to explain. "I've been in love with Catherine since I was fresh out of uni' and started working for her. Meeting you has put that in perspective for me. I realise now, most of that was hero worship – your sister is the extreme best at what she does. Her mind calculates and reconfigures in a way I have no hope of ever matching – and not being big headed, but I'm pretty damn good too."

Yes you are, and I'm an idiot!

Laughing at his trumpet blowing, Caroline brings their joined hands up to her lips. "Ok, so I'm not a substitute," she grins up at him, "but let's keep this casual. My heart won't survive another breakup."

Returning her kiss to their joined hands, Ben agrees to Caroline's terms. "I can do casual," and they both laugh as he gives her a Boy Scouts salute, "honest."

"I'll get dressed and we can eat in the hotel dining room, if you're up for it?"

He grins suggestively and waggles his eyebrows. "You know me, baby, I'm always up for anything," and Ben receives a slap to his thigh for his trouble.

Less than half an hour later, they walk arm in arm in to the hotel dining room. "Ms Thornton," the Maître d' welcomes her warmly, and it is obvious that he knows of her fame as a pianist. He signals one of his headwaiters over and asks him to show the couple to a specific table. "For your privacy," he bows his head and includes Ben in his salutation.

"Wow," Ben raises an eyebrow as they are shown to the best table, "how the other half live, hey?"

"It has its drawbacks, I can assure you." But Caroline doesn't seem to be bothered by them just now. "It also has its uses – did you see that poster in reception, the one about a fundraising event in aid of a young local girl with Cerebral Palsy?"

"Yes, I know her family – they're trying to get her in to the Meyo Clinic. But it's damnably expensive, and then there's the family living expenses, even basic accommodation and groceries won't come cheap." He gives a resigned sigh. "The parents, Steve and Gail Harrington, will be grateful for whatever they can raise. They've been told they can be taught the techniques that the institute uses, enough so that they can implement them when they get back home."

"They sound dedicated." Caroline frowns in contemplation then asks Ben to excuse her for a couple of minutes. "Would you mind ordering for me - I'm not vegetarian and I'll try most things at least once." She smiles briefly then turns and walks away, leaving Ben confused and bewildered.

Walking out to the main reception area, Caroline reads the poster again then makes her way over to the desk. "Could I speak to the manager please," she asks the receptionist who promptly pales and looks mortified. "There's no problem, I assure you, but I would like to have a word about the fundraising event advertised on that poster," and Caroline points over to it.

"Oh, of course, Ms Thornton, I'll just get her for you."

Poor little thing probably thought I was going to cause a stink about some complaint or other. She's seen Clive do it a time or two, and vowed never to copy his high-handed behaviour. *He was always the big 'I am'. Funny, I don't think I really thought of that before.*

"Ms Thornton, how may I help you," the manageress asks from somewhere just above Caroline's navel.

"Oh, err, I was rather hoping I could help you," she smiles affably. "Or at least, the family the fundraiser is for."

The manageress nods considering this. "Did you wish to make a donation?"

"Actually, yes," Caroline beams as another thought strikes her. "But if you could give me a moment I may be able to do more than that."

Moving to one side Caroline contacts her dad on her mobile. "It's such a lovely cause, and it's to help a local family." Listening to her dad's advice about how to set things up and what he will do from his end, Caroline is chuffed to bits that he is so willing to help. "Will you come, dad?" For a couple of long seconds there is silence on the other end of the line, and then her dad confirms that he will. "Oh, dad, thank you. I love you so much, and I know you and Catherine will get on really well; she's lovely dad, really lovely."

We can be a real family. After all this time alone, Catherine will have a family to care for her.

Turning back to the manageress, Caroline is full of enthusiasm. "If the family agree, I will give a benefit performance here in the hotel to help raise some funds.

There will be absolutely no charge for my part and my dad thinks he can get some big names to either take part or just come along and make a donation."

The manageress is almost speechless. "Well, that's very kind of you, Ms Thornton, very kind indeed." Smiling broadly, she nods her head and clasps her hands together. "I'll contact the family right now, but I can tell you already they will agree and be very grateful for all your help." Shaking Caroline's hand, the manageress goes off to inform the family and make a few necessary arrangements.

The cause is definitely worth any effort I have to make to give the best benefit performance I can arrange, but it will also give the family a reason to come together. It wasn't my first thought, but I think it could work. I have to make it work!

Caroline takes a deep breath and returns to the dining room where Ben is patiently waiting. "You look buzzed," he smiles and frowns quizzically. "What have you been up to?"

Explaining about the benefit that she's just offered to do, Caroline also mentions the fact that her dad has agreed to come. "So dad and Catherine will finally meet," she grins excitedly. "I know my dad's really nervous; I didn't think he was going to come at first. And I'm sure

Catherine will be nervous too, which is why I don't propose to tell her until the day dad decides to come." She looks anxiously at Ben. "Do you think that's a good idea – I just think Catherine will panic and fly off into a rage, and she may do or say something that we'll all regret?" *Oh, please, please let this work. It has to work. It just has to.*

Nodding his agreement, Ben purses his lips and considers the idea. "I think you're dead right about Catherine – that's exactly the kind of reaction she's likely to have."

The waiter arrives with their starters, and Caroline gives an appreciative sniff at the bowl of beef and vegetable broth that is set in front of her. Smiling up at the waiter she says, "This smells delicious, thank you."

"This wine is pretty good, too," Ben sips appreciatively. "So, what shall we drink too?"

Tilting her head to consider Ben, Caroline holds up her wine glass, "To friendship, and your partnership, may you and Catherine have many happy years together," she giggles.

"Hey, Colson, Ben, how are you both?" Josh Palmer is smiling widely and striding towards their table.

Wow! Serious wow! You know the most gorgeous men, sis'.

Ben makes to correct Josh's understandable mistake but Caroline gives his shins a quick kick under the table. "How are you?" she smiles warmly. "Won't you join us for a glass of excellent wine?" Steady, girl, just remember you're Catherine now – not Caroline.

Raising his eyebrows at her polite and sociable greeting, Josh pulls up a chair and signals the waiter for a wine glass. "So, are you guys celebrating something?"

"We certainly are," Caroline grins, and Josh can't help but grin back, "Ben has accepted an offer to become a fully-fledged partner in the firm."

Slapping Ben on the back, Josh raises his now full glass of wine. "Congratulations, old man, and no doubt thoroughly deserved." He turns back to Caroline. "You've always said how much you value Ben's skills; I suppose this just goes to show how much." Raising his glass to both of them he says, "Here's to a long and lucrative partnership, cheers."

"Cheers." Caroline and Ben both echo and the three of them clink glasses.

Chatting easily, Caroline listens intently and chimes in when she knows she can do so appropriately. Though, when they start to talk about the new security upgrade and programming that Compusafe has just installed at

Josh's company, Caroline has to sit back and try not to look bored.

"Ms Thornton," the hotel Manageress is beaming as she walks towards their table. "I thought I should let you know immediately…," then falters as if only just realising that Caroline is not dining alone, "…oh, I'm so sorry. I was so excited I didn't think." And she looks at the two men who have now stopped talking and are looking at her quizzically.

"It's quite alright, I assure you," Caroline tells the floundering woman. "Now, what were you going to let me know?" *Oh well, fun while it lasted.*

Continuing to look a little hesitant, some of the Manageress's former excitement makes itself known in her voice. "I have just come from speaking to the family and the owner of The Lovett Hotel," she declares with no little satisfaction. "The family are thrilled, of course, and asked me to extend their heartfelt thanks and appreciation." Clasping her hands together tightly, the Manageress is barely able to contain her excitement. "Mr Travis Lovett, the owner of The Lovett Hotel has declared that he will personally pick up your hotel bill, and has insisted that any cost involved with the benefit be put through the hotel for his attention."

Good lord — sounds like the man from on-high has spoken. Still, he certainly has a generous spirit.

"That is a very generous offer," Caroline smiles. *But so over the top and controlling. Well, this little lady can take care of herself, thank you very much.* "Perhaps you could thank Mr Lovett for me, and explain that while I am happy for him to offer assistance with the cost of the benefit itself, I can take care of my own hotel bill."

The Manageress blusters so profusely that Caroline imagines steam might come out of her ears at any second. "I...I...well...I don't know...I mean...," her cheeks redden brightly, her eyes wide and askance, "...Mr Travis, he was quite insistent." Then she seems to realise her mistake. "I mean to say, I believe Mr Travis sees his offer as a way of donating to the cause."

Nodding her head in understanding, Caroline tries to put the woman at her ease while sticking to her decision. "I'm sure Mr Lovett is a very generous man and, as I said, I will certainly be happy to accept any help he may wish to offer with the cost of setting the benefit itself up." *He's probably an irascible old man used to getting his own way. Or maybe you're just a grumpy cow who's down on the male species and seeing the worst in all of them. Shit!*

Realising that she cannot push the issue without being rude to a valued guest, the Manageress gives a polite nod of her head and assures Caroline that she will pass on her feelings on the matter.

Josh is frowning deeply, having listened to their conversation he has no idea what Colson is up to and also has no idea why they addressed her as Ms Thornton. "What are you up to, Colson – and why did that woman address you as Ms Thornton?" He looks over at Ben, who is now smiling to himself, and feels even more at a loss.

"Rumbled," Caroline smiles at Ben. "Oh well. I suppose I'll have to confess now." Enjoying Josh's obvious confusion, Caroline takes a sip of wine then begins the explanation. "My name is Caroline Thornton; I am a concert pianist and have offered to perform in a benefit in aid of a local family who have a daughter in need of treatment abroad."

"Bullshit!" Josh gasps before he can stop himself. Turning to look at Ben his frown deepens, "What the hell is going on?"

"You have just met Catherine's sister, Caroline," and Ben turns to raise his glass to her, "her identical twin sister," he confirms when Josh still looks confused. *And the most lovely creature on God's green earth!*

Sitting back in his seat, Josh regards Caroline with obvious interest. "I have actually heard of you," he tells her, "and I believe my parents have recordings of your concerts." He continues to consider her, "But I have never heard Colson speak of having a sister, let alone an identical twin sister."

She hasn't mentioned you either, but here you sit like an Adonis fallen from heaven. "We both had no idea the other existed," Caroline informs him frankly. "We were brought up separately. Me by our father and Catherine by our mother, and in their wisdom they decided it would be less hurtful for us both to grow up oblivious of the other's existence." *But no amount of distance or secrecy has been able to keep us apart.*

"That's amazing, truly amazing." Josh shakes his head as if to clear it. "So, are you staying with Colson and Logan – I presume you are both desperately trying to catch up on all those missing years."

You have no idea. The loss is hard to bear, and there is no replacing those lost years. But we will find out why they were stolen from us, and who was responsible for tearing two little girls apart.

"I did stay with them, at first," Caroline smiles softly, "but I didn't want to intrude on young love." *And I needed some time and space to come to terms with our mum's murder, and the fact that poor Catherine had suffered through it all alone.* "I'm staying here, now," and she waves a hand to indicate the sumptuous surroundings, "the natives are friendly and the accommodations are excellent." She smiles mischievously at Ben, "At least we think so."

Josh's eyebrow cocks up and he looks questioningly at Ben. "You are staying here, too?"

His obvious incredulity irks Ben. "Sometimes," and he smiles suggestively at Caroline. *You're not the only eligible bastard on the planet, Palmer!*

"Well, it's been a real pleasure meeting you," Josh gets to his feet, and taking Caroline's hand raises it to his lips. "My parent's would love to meet you, also – would you come to dinner one evening this week?"

Smooth. Very smooth. "I'd love to. Just leave a message with the date and time at reception – they'll see that I get it." *You have lovely eyes, and you're still holding my hand. Are you flirting with me, Josh Palmer – to wind Ben up, or are you really interested? Hmm, I suppose we'll see soon enough.*

Their main course arrives and Josh is forced to take his leave, much to Ben's evident relief. Once the waiters have disappeared he makes his feelings plain. "Don't feel obliged to go, Caroline," he tells her, sounding a little belligerent and even a little whiney, "Palmer is a nice enough chap in small doses, but he can be a bit high and mighty when he wants something."

About to put a forkful of prime beef steak in to her mouth, Caroline stops and asks, "And you think he wants me?" *Interesting.*

Ben almost chokes in his haste to swallow the contents of his mouth. "Are you kidding – who wouldn't want you?"

Clive. He never really wanted me.

The question is posed more as a statement of fact and acts as a balm on her badly bruised heart.

The following week passes in a blur of activity. Caroline, as well as continuing her daily piano practice, is busy working with her dad to organise the charity Benefit.

"Dad, that's amazing," Caroline tells him when she hears about the big names he has managed to confirm as attending and even performing. "Have you told The Lovett management or do you want me to do that?"

By the end of the call, Caroline is really pumped and goes to tell The Lovett Hotel management that they now have a major event on their hands. Only three weeks to go and she still has a lot to do.

Thankfully her dinner at the Palmer's isn't until the following Monday; Mr and Mrs Palmer being away in the country with friends until Sunday.

"Catherine, hi," Caroline grins in to her mobile, "I've just gotten off the phone with dad and he's arranged for some of the most amazing prestigious people to attend and even perform at the charity Benefit."

However, Catherine, although thrilled that her sister's plans are going well, is ploughed under with the move to her new office premises. "Sorry, sorry, sorry, I should have made time to come and help," Caroline laments when she realises. "Do you want me to come over; I could put this on hold for the rest of today?"

But Catherine won't hear of it. Logan, as well as already having the premises on his books has pushed through the paperwork on the cash sale and got some of his own men to help with the heavy moving. "Ok, I can hear the chaos in the background, but don't forget I want a guided tour as soon as you're settled in?"

Dressed in a rust coloured blouse with its top three buttons undone and a cream calf length pencil skirt, Caroline cuts a fine figure as she strides purposefully towards the reception desk in her three inch heels.

"Oh, Ms Thornton," the Manageress greets her, ignoring all Caroline's requests that she use her given name, "I was hoping to catch you after your practice session."

"Is there something wrong to do with the Benefit?" Caroline asks alarmed at the thought of having to cancel or postpone some of the very big names her father has told her about. *Oh, shit!*

"No, no, the event is still as scheduled," the tiny woman beams. "In fact, Mr Travis himself has asked to meet with you at your earliest convenience. He rarely takes visitors," she adds in lowered tones, "would you be free to see him now?"

So, the old coot wants a visitor. Perhaps he isn't able to get out much. "Now would be fine," Caroline agrees pleasantly, and is shown to a private lift.

"Mr Travis will be expecting you. This lift serves only Mr Travis's private penthouse."

Stepping inside the smaller, swankier lift, Caroline observes her reflection in the mirror opposite and deems herself suitably attired for taking a midmorning meeting with the elderly owner of the hotel.

However, when the lift door opens, Caroline isn't greeted by a doddering retiree, but a giant of a man with a physique to match Logan's. *Fuck!*

"Please, take a seat," his large hand sweeps to indicate a plush leather settee. "Thank you for giving up some of your valuable time to see me."

Taking a seat as requested, Caroline finds herself almost cricking her neck to look up at him. But he remains standing, half in shadow by the tall windows. "Won't you join me?" she asks, but might as well not have spoken for all the notice he takes.

"I have asked for both tea and coffee to be sent up, as I was informed that you enjoy both equally."

His dark brown voice has her mesmerised, as do his beautiful blue eyes. He wears his chestnut hair in shiny waves to his shoulders, not unlike her father's she muses. *Jesus, this man is...Well, he's bloody damned gorgeous is what he is!*

"Ms Thornton?" he asks, and she realises she hasn't heard a word he said.

"Oh, oh," she stammers like a babbling teenager, "I'm so sorry, I was lost in thought." *I was lost in you, actually. Christ, could I get lost in you.*

"No doubt you have a lot to think about," he barely smiles and his eyes shift to the young waitress standing by a trolley laden with tea, coffee and small sandwiches with the crusts removed and a silver platter of finger cakes. "Would you like tea or coffee?" he asks again and she plumps for black tea.

After the waitress has served her drink, Caroline refuses the offer of food. Her stomach is churning uncomfortably and the last thing she wants is to throw up in front of this god of a man. *He already thinks I'm an air-*

headed female; let's not give him anything else to look down his glorious nose at me for.

"You wanted to meet with me," Caroline decided to put her business head back on, "was there something particular you wanted to discuss?"

He continues to regard her in silence, until eventually Caroline actually squirms in her seat. "Why are you putting yourself to so much trouble for a family you know nothing about?"

In other words, what am I getting out of it? Tilting her head she frowns up at him. "I could ask you the same thing," she states more confidently than she feels. "Why offer to pick up the considerable tab on a charity Benefit for a little girl you've never met?" *Ok, that was a guess, but according to your own staff you rarely leave this ivory tower.*

Regarding her steadily his full lips finally pull in to a smile that could put even the sun in the shade.

Holy shit, you are so damned hot!

"Touché, Ms Thornton, but I'm not the one putting all the effort in to organising the event."

"And you can't imagine anyone doing such a thing simply because they want to help someone in need?" *What a sceptic.*

Again, he regards her steadily. "Having met you, I would have to say that I am no longer convinced that you are positioning yourself for the obvious publicity that an event like this will generate."

Caroline gasps. "Well, why don't you say what you really think," she tells him, getting to her feet and placing the cup she wants to throw at him carefully on a nearby table. "But you are right about the publicity," she tells him, and smiles as he nods his acceptance of being right about her, "I fully intend to court the press and I'll be making a few television appearances – that should really put my face on the media map, don't you think?" *You might look like a fallen angel, but your heart is solid stone. Bloody men. Gits, all of them!*

Crossing the room she is stunned when she reaches out to press for the lift and his hand takes hers to stop her. *How the hell did you cross the room so fast and so quietly?*

"I can see I've upset you," he croons softly, his lovely voice strumming a response from somewhere deep inside of her, "that wasn't my intent, I assure you."

She turns to ask him just exactly what his intent was then gasps with horrified shock at his beautiful marred face. "No…," the plaintiff cry escapes her unnoticed and her hand flies instinctively to cup his badly scarred cheek.

At first he is stunned in to immobility, but then he firmly takes her hand from his face and turns away. "I don't need your pity, Ms Thornton. I asked you here to ascertain your motives – I've done that, now you can go."

Her lips tremble and her lovely eyes fill with tears. Pressing the call button Caroline waits quietly for the lift, not daring to turn and look at Travis. The door opens and she steps in then turns and their eyes lock just as the first tear falls.

With a heavy heart, she watches the door slide shut and the tears fall with terrible abandon.

Chapter Six

Pulling up on Logan's drive, Caroline tries to rub the throb in her temple away, but it's stubborn and persistent.

When Logan opens the front door to greet her, he can see the pain behind Caroline's eyes, but not the cause for it. "Are you ok?" he asks reaching out to put a gentle hand to her forehead. "You're not sickening for something?"

Shaking her head, Caroline doesn't trust her voice to answer him. Then allows him to pull her in to a brotherly hug and wallows in the safety of family. "Thanks, bro', I needed that."

"What's wrong, what's happened?" Catherine isn't the least bit jealous to see her sister in Logan's arms, but concern and fear flood through her.

Turning to Catherine, seeing her sister's concern and, yes love, Caroline goes from a brother's embrace to a sister's and this time the floodgates open. "Oh, sis' I've been such an idiot." *And then some! Shit! Shit! Shit!*

Looking over Caroline's shoulder, Catherine's big eyes plead with Logan for help. She loves her sister, without a doubt, but she doesn't know the first thing about comforting one and Mrs Baines, a treasure in all things, has already gone home.

"Come on now," Logan embraces both women and, before gently pulling them apart, places an understanding kiss on Catherine's forehead. "Let's go through to the sitting-room and you can tell us all about it." But after looking at both girls faces he decides to change tack. "Ok, let me get you both settled in the sitting-room with a drink, and then maybe a little sister-to-sister talk would help?"

Caroline's bottom lip is still trembling precariously. "Thanks Logan."

"Hey, I was bro' a minute ago," he chastises, and gets the smile he wanted.

"I've always wanted a big brother," she looks up at Logan and then to Catherine, "I'm so lucky to have you both." And before the flood can start again, he guides them in to the sitting-room and hands them both a large glass of wine.

The minute the lounge door closes, Catherine wades in. "Is this Ben's fault? What did that fucker do? I'll knock him from here to next week if he caused this?" *Partner! I'll give him partner! Fucker!*

But Caroline shakes her head despairingly. "It isn't Ben's fault, it's mine," she tells her and lets go of a long shaky breath. "You know I've been seeing Ben...well, more than seeing, really," and Catherine blushes but nods her head. "Well, at first it was just fun – I told Ben right off the blocks that it had to be a casual friendship, nothing deep and meaningful."

"But he broke the rules and got serious?" Catherine asks, now suddenly feeling sorry for Ben.

At first Caroline shakes her head then nods in agreement. "I haven't seen Ben today – he's been busy with the move and then I told him I was coming over here for some family time."

Jesus, what the fuck am I supposed to do? My sister needs me and I don't have a clue what she's talking about!

"So you and Ben didn't have a fallout - a fight over him becoming too serious?"

"No, no... Oh, Catherine, I'm a terrible person!" And to Catherine's horror the tears start to fall in earnest again.

Logan! What in blue blazes do I do now! "Caroline, please…," she pulls her sister in to her arms and tentatively pats her back the way she's seen mothers in the street doing to calm a crying child. *It always seems to work for them.* "I can't help you if you don't tell me what's wrong – if it isn't Ben…then who…or what?"

Reaching for a tissue, Caroline tries to stem the tears. *This is ridiculous. I'm ridiculous, and that's just what Catherine and Logan will think if I tell them about Travis!* "I'm a mess," Caroline states the obvious and takes a sip of her wine, "I should never have got involved with Ben – it was just a knee-jerk reaction to Clive."

"Well, I have to admit I did think it was a bit soon," Catherine observes. "But then, what do I know about relationships, I've never had any!"

Having decided not to spill the beans about Travis, Caroline now needs to think up a convincing story as to why she is upset. "I know I got myself in to this, but now I have no idea how to get myself out of it," she tells Catherine. "Ben has been great, if a little too caring – but I need some space to get my head together." *Which is true – it just isn't the real reason I need to break up with Ben. Bloody hell!*

"What do you think he'll do…," she asks Catherine nervously, "…will he be gutted or do you think he'll just take it on the chin and move on?"

Bloody buggering hell, not again! The poor bloke gets a knock-back from one sister then gets tossed aside by the other. Fuck me! "Perhaps you should hold off on telling Ben until you've had time to calm down and think this all through rationally," Catherine advises, and silently congratulates herself on managing to give such sound advice. *There, this sister lark isn't so hard.*

A knock on the sitting-room door signals Logan's return. "Dinner is on the table, ladies. Perhaps a good meal will help put things in to perspective."

The girls rise, and arm in arm take their unfinished wine through to the conservatory.

Once seated, Catherine decides to change the subject completely. "I've been doing some digging, like we talked about. You know, about mum and dad's break up and why we got split up," she explains when Caroline looks blank.

"Oh!" And Caroline's bottom lips starts to tremble again. "How selfish of me, I haven't given poor mum a thought."

But Catherine panics at the thought of battling another onslaught of tears. "No, no more tears," she tells Caroline firmly. "Jesus, Caroline, will you stop beating yourself up over everything. You've been helping that poor young girl's family by organising some posh charity do. Which, by the way, I'd have run a million miles from." *Christ, all those people, all that hand shaking – all that kiss arse and cow-towing. Yuk! No, big fucking yuk!*

"It's really not so bad," Caroline takes a shuddering breath and swallows back the tears. "Dad's been a big help. He's lined up a few mega-rich attendee's and talked a few big names in to performing and donating their usual fee to the cause." Watching Catherine's reaction to the mention of their dad, she continues. "He's even started getting the event some free publicity on national radio. I think that's why some of the big name performers agreed to come. It'll be great PR." Frowning, she remembers Travis's suggestion that she is giving all her time and efforts for the same reason and feels guilty for thinking it of others.

"I suppose all that means that it's going well, right?" Catherine asks hopefully.

"It is indeed," and Caroline smiles for the first time. "Now, tell me what you've found out about mum?"

Logan continues with his meal until he almost chokes on a mouthful. "You've been hacking in to your mother's medical files – are you completely off your trolley?" he asks, using a phrase he's picked up from Catherine.

Wafting his concerns aside with an airy wave of her hand, Catherine explains, "When we were looking for mum's murderer I did a lot of hacking to get info I couldn't get any other way." Turning back to Logan, she adds, "I didn't get caught then and I won't now. So either cool off or don't listen, that's just the start of it." *Shit. Maybe he won't go full on ballistic with Caroline here.*

"You…err…you get in to other people's computers?" Caroline asks not sure if she has understood correctly. "How?" *I didn't know that was even possible.*

"Well…," she begins to explain after taking a side-long under-the-lashes look at Logan, "…there's no point going in to all the technical details, but suffice to say I use a programme that I wrote to get in and out without leaving any trace behind."

"And it's that simple?" Caroline's eyebrows arch and she glances over at Logan. He doesn't look like he thinks it's that simple. *Fuck. What is Catherine getting herself in to?*

"In theory…" Catherine begins to explain again, but is cut off by Logan.

"In theory anything is possible," he exclaims with admirable restraint. "But the fact is, as brilliant as you are, Catherine, even you can make mistakes. The consequences of which would be catastrophic – both personally and for your business!"

Going first pale at the thought of her business reputation being sullied, then red hot at his obvious lack of faith in her, Catherine bristles. "I'm not an idiot, I'm thorough and methodical so that mistakes don't happen," she tells him hotly.

"Hey, hey," Caroline holds up a hand for peace. "I didn't come here to start you two off on a row. That would really top my wonderful day off," she states sarcastically. *Why did I even get out of bed this morning – I obviously can't do anything right!*

Getting up from the table, Caroline strolls down to the cosy end of the conservatory and makes herself comfortable in one of the padded seats. The night is just starting to draw in and she enjoys the view of the garden in twilight. "Sorry," she says when Catherine comes to join her carrying another large glass of wine for each of them. "I feel like I can't do right for doing wrong today. I haven't a clue what to do about Ben – he said he could do casual, but I'm not so sure." *Neither can I, if I'm really honest. I was just on the rebound.*

"Forget about Ben for tonight, he's an adult and made his own choices," Catherine assures her, more confidently than she really feels. "Now, about mum," Catherine turns to see if Logan is within earshot then turns back to Caroline, "I got in to Erin Vandivier's bank account…," she begins then has to shush Caroline quickly when she gasps out loud. "Keep it down, you've seen what Logan's like about these things. He'll blow a fuse if he knows I've hacked the Bank of Sheriton!" *And then I'll blow a fuse because he'll nag me about it! When did everything get so bloody complicated?*

"Catherine, I know you're the best — Ben told me as much — but please be careful. I can't lose you, too, and to a prison cell at that!" Caroline rubs her hands over her tired face. "I don't know why I'm so damned tired all of a sudden."

"Couldn't be because you've been working your flaming arse off on this charity thing, I suppose." The sarcasm is not lost on Caroline and they look at each other and laugh almost hysterically.

"Now that's a sound I could listen to all evening," Logan grins as he joins them, taking a seat near Catherine. "I've always loved your laugh, now I get to hear it in stereo." And they all give a relieved laugh that the tension has passed.

"I shouldn't really drink this," Caroline looks at her untouched glass of wine, "I need to drive back."

"Not tonight you're not," Logan states firmly. "The room you were in is already made up. Mrs Baines believes in being prepared."

"I'd like to be polite and make at least a token protest," she grimaces wryly, "but I'd actually love to stay. There's nothing like family when the heart is aching." *And you are my family. I feel as sure of that as I do about loving Travis.*

"That's settled then. Now, why don't you two take a walk in the garden while I read the Financial Times in peace with my feet up?"

They know he's just trying to give them some space and privacy, and are grateful for his consideration.

"Is there a pipe and slippers I can get you to go with that newspaper?" Catherine grins cheekily.

"I'll give you pipe and slippers, madam." Leaping out of his chair he catches Catherine around the waist and she squeals with laughter. Caroline makes a discrete exit and walks to sit by the fish pond.

"You two are so great together," she tells Catherine a couple of minutes later.

Blushing madly, Catherine has to agree. "He wants me to move in permanently. He asked me to marry him, and I sort of said yes, but the thought scares me half to death," she confesses on a long sigh.

"I'm scared too," Caroline admits. "Just the thought of giving my heart to another man, ever, is terrifying. Clive really did a number on me."

"Anyway," Caroline shrugs herself out of her morbid contemplations, "you were telling me about your progress with our little mystery. What did you find out about Erin Vandivier?"

"Oh, yes," Catherine is suddenly all fired up. "I did find a number of anomalies. Like payments made out to mum for a hundred pounds here and fifty pounds there. All of which was paid back," she states proudly, knowing how her mum felt about debt, "and all around the time when her medical records at The Brantings Surgery came to an abrupt halt." Contemplating the fish swimming round and round in the pond; Catherine tries and fails to come up with a reason for the halt in medical records. "We always went to the doctors at The Brantings. At least, I did, I suppose I just assumed mum did too."

"And you don't think they could have been wiped?" Caroline speculates, only just beginning to realise that any such thing might be possible.

Looking stunned, Catherine stares at her sister. "Fuck me! Some computer whiz I am," she splutters, her arms flying out in all directions.

Then a splash in the pond makes both girls look and scream in unison.

Logan comes dashing to their assistance then laughs when he sees them both splashed with pond-water. "Charlie, that was naughty," he wags a finger at one of the largest fish Catherine has ever seen.

"You've got a friggin' shark living in that bloody pond and it damn near took a piece out of me!" Catherine exclaims angrily. "So instead of telling Charlie what a naughty boy he is, go and get a sodding gun and shoot the fucker!"

Logan doubles up with laughter, and even Caroline is finding it difficult to smother a grin. "Poor old Charlie, you wouldn't hurt a fly, would you boy."

"Look…look…see, I told you he's vicious," and she punches Logan on the arm as Charlie jumps almost clear of the water when he waves his hand over it. "See, and he's a big bastard, too!" *Fuck me! Must be some kind of damn mutant. I never heard of a goldfish growing that big!*

Tears of mirth are gathering in Logan's eyes as he swings Catherine up and around in the air. "No wonder I love you," he laughs, but Catherine is not in the mood.

"Get off me, you lunatic!" She gives his arm another punch, but Logan barely registers it.

"He just thought you were going to feed him," Logan explains as he sets Catherine back on her feet. "If you sit there long enough he expects you to throw him a few pellets, that's all." He reaches over and presses the plunger on the front of a container. Out of the hole in the bottom, a portion of pellets fall in to Logan's waiting hand. "Here now, just throw a few in," he encourages, but Catherine backs off warily.

"You first, big guy," she tells him. "You're the one on first name terms with jaws."

Caroline can't stem her laughter any longer and earns a scowl from her sister. "It's just a Koi Carp," she grins easily, "dad used to keep them before we started touring."

"I've never heard of…coy…whatever it was you said," Catherine begins to watch with interest as Logan feeds the huge fish. "I thought goldfish lived in ponds?"

"They do," Logan confirms as he gives the last of the pellets to Charlie. "They're just not the only type of fish to live in ponds." Sliding his palms over each other to brush off the pellet dust, Logan looks over at Caroline. "You look all in. Why don't you get an early night – the world might seem a brighter place after a good night's sleep?"

Feeling the weight of the world on her shoulders, Caroline agrees. "If you really don't mind," and she looks over to Catherine, receiving a shake of her head in reply, "then I will go up. You're right, bro'," she tells him and reaches up to give Logan a peck on his cheek, "a good night's sleep is probably the answer." After giving Catherine a goodnight hug, she gratefully makes her way up to bed.

Sleep claims her the minute her head touches the pillow. Her dreams are scattered and somehow frantic. Flitting from the scene in Travis's penthouse to a raging argument with Ben, she then sees herself crying on the hotel bed, seemingly inconsolable.

Waking up with a start, Caroline sits up in bed then lays back down and falls straight back into her troubling dreams. She is in his penthouse again, watching him watching her. He looks sullen and a shadow of cruelty lay behind his eyes. She is afraid of him, but when he walks towards her she doesn't back away.

"So brave for one so scared," he taunts her, reaching out a hand to stroke her cheek. "How lovely and soft and perfect your face is," his dark brown voice is little more than a whisper. "Unlike my own," he tells her then suddenly lifts his long hair to reveal the terrible scars beneath. "Not a pretty sight," he sneers when she gasps with shock.

No! No! No!

He jerks away and she feels the loss. *No, don't leave me.* "It isn't the scars that are ugly, it's the act that put them there," she tells him. *And the ugliness that has grown within.*

His expression is uncertain when he turns back to her, and then the cruel shadow cloaks his eyes again. "So, you don't think I'm ugly?" His words are a whispered challenge spoken so close to her lips that she can feel the warmth of his breath.

If you only knew how you make me feel.

A hand fists in the short locks of hair at the nape of Caroline's neck and tug her head back painfully. Her milk white neck seems to hold him spellbound, and she actually thinks he might bite her like a vampire. But when his lips touch her skin they are soft and warm, unlike the hot flames that flare beneath them and spread through her veins like a brush fire.

I can't breathe. If you don't kiss me soon I'll die of this need.

Travis moves his lips up to her ear, tasting her milky skin with great relish as he does. "Shall I kiss your beautiful lips, Caroline? Will beauty allow the beast one taste of the forbidden fruit?"

Not a beast. You're not a beast!

Her head is thrashing side to side on her pillow, as Caroline burns up with fever. "You're not a beast," she calls out, and doesn't realise that Catherine is wiping her face with a cold damp sponge.

"Logan, she's delirious – what do we do?" Catherine asks when Logan comes back in to Caroline's bedroom.

"I've rung Doctor Goss, he'll be here within thirty," he tells her. "He said to keep doing what you're doing and he'll get here as quick as he can."

Not fifteen minutes later, Doctor Goss sits on Caroline's bed and takes her temperature. Looking over at Logan, he tries to convey the seriousness without alarming Catherine. "I think it might be best to err on the side of caution and call an ambulance," he pronounces, then pats Catherine's hand when she gasps with fear. "Not to worry. Not to worry. I'm fairly sure it's just a bug she's picked up on top of being worn out." He looks to Logan again. "You did say you thought she had been overdoing things of late?"

Nodding, Logan moves to put a comforting hand on Catherine's shoulder. "Yes, she's been putting together a charity benefit for a young local girl. It's all she's talked about for days."

"Ah," the Doctor lifts a finger in the air, "I think I know her. Young Chloe Harrington, is it?" And Logan nods to confirm it is. "A more deserving family I've yet to meet. They have a boy, too, Kyle, a couple of years older than Chloe. His mum tells me he looks after and plays with Chloe all the time - loves her to bits, apparently." Getting to his feet, Doctor Goss looks over at Catherine, "Keep up the good work, young lady. That's doing her the world of good – although I'd strip everything off that modesty will allow and put a fan on her if you have one."

Logan takes his cue from the Doctor following him out of the bedroom and pulling the door closed behind him. "Ok, now tell me the worst?" Logan demands without beating about the bush.

"There's a very real possibility that it could be viral meningitis." Doctor Goss chews on his bottom lip. "Had a case of it a couple of days ago and another about a week since." He shakes his head. "So far we can't find a common link, but let's not jump the gun. You go back in to Catherine and help her to stay calm, I'll call the ambulance and get them here as a priority case." Patting Logan on the shoulder he says, "Try not to worry too soon, it could be something or nothing at all. We won't know for sure until the tests are performed and the results are back."

For the next week Catherine spends each day at her sister's bedside, and would have spent the nights there too if Logan hadn't put his foot down. "I've given the ward Sister all of our contact numbers, if there is any change they'll let us know."

When Catherine had tried to protest Logan used tough love. "Unless you want to end up in a bed alongside your sister, you'll do as I ask and come home to get some proper rest and some nutritious food, instead of the junk you've been picking at."

The first night, Caroline didn't wake at all, just tossed and turned in her sleep. She has a couple of intravenous infusions going in through a central line the doctors have placed in her neck. It has four lumens, one of which has been wrapped in a sterile dressing in case she needs it for parenteral nutrition.

Her temperature is still very high despite the IV antibiotics she is receiving along with the IV Paracetamol.

A gentle hand strokes Caroline's damp hair back from her pale face. "You cried for me, I don't believe anyone else ever has." The dark voice comes and goes along with his touch, and Caroline enjoys her delirious dreams of Travis.

She hears him reading to her, not quite able to hang on to the words long enough to make out what it's about. But the sound of his soft brown tones comfort and sooth her. Reaching out a hand in to the darkness she calls his name, "Travis," and feels her hand held safe and warm in his. A tremulous smile tugs at her lips, "I love you, Travis," and then she falls back into oblivion and darkness.

On day five her eyes finally open to a too bright light and she squeezes her eyes closed again in protest.

"Caroline, wake up, honey," Catherine begs and gives her sister's shoulders a gentle shake. "Caroline, open your eyes," she demands more firmly, and is rewarded when her sister's lids flutter open. Moving to the door she calls for a nurse. "Everything is going to be alright, now, Caroline," but she can't help crying.

"Then why are you crying?" Caroline asks when she can finally speak.

"Because I'm an idiot," Catherine tells her then bends over the bed to give her sister a huge hug. "You scared me. Don't do that again!"

"Ok, sis'," Caroline strokes the back of Catherine's head, "no worries, I'm fine." *Was it the drugs or did I just have the best dreams ever?*

<u>Chapter Seven</u>

Back in her hotel room, after two-days convalescence with Catherine and Logan, Caroline actually feels like she's raring to go. The first thing she did after getting out of the hospital was to phone her dad. Her mobile had been locked and Catherine had no way of contacting him.

He'd been frantic, of course, offering to catch the next available flight from London. But she had managed to put him off. Not that she hadn't been tempted to let him come it might have been the perfect opportunity for him to meet Catherine. However, Caroline preferred to be fully back on her feet to referee that meeting, just in case it went badly.

Her calf-length blue chiffon dress hangs loose on Caroline's now too thin frame. But there isn't much she can do about it now; she frowns at her reflection before making her way down to the lounge for her first practice session since she took ill.

"Damn!" She has played the same piece twice and both times has made the same mistake.

"Give yourself time," a familiar voice speaks from the shadows. "You'll make yourself ill again if you push too hard."

"How do you know I've been ill?" she asks then some of her dreams come more clearly back to her. *Were they dreams, or were you really there? No, you couldn't have been. Just some drug induced delusions, but they were damned good ones!*

"I may not go out much, but I get to hear pretty much all of what goes on in the local district," he informs her. "Now, try some basic warm up techniques, you're trying to run before you can walk."

She frowns in his general direction. "Getting a tad bossy aren't we," Caroline tells him. But inside her heart is skipping with joy.

After half an hour of chords and exercise pieces, she breaks out in to one of her favourite compositions. Lost in her music Caroline doesn't notice Travis move out of the shadows to her right side. When she goes in to her second piece, she feels his presence without having seen him and looks up to find him watching her intently.

"Don't stop," he tells her, and moves to sit by her side as Caroline continues to let her fingers fly across the black and white keys. "I love to listen to you play. You have a true gift, Caroline, one that brings a lot of joy to a great many people."

Do you remember what joy is?

"How do you hear me from up in your ivory tower?" she asks not looking at him.

His smile is evident in his voice. "I have ways of being around and not being seen," he tells her cryptically.

"What, like secret passages and lift shafts," she teases and giggles at the thought.

Her laughter makes him laugh, too - not as exuberantly as Caroline, but enough for him to recognise the strangeness of the sound. He hasn't laughed in a very long time, nor even smiled, he realises sadly.

His sad eyes regard her as she continues to play. "You've lost a lot of weight, Caroline. Please be careful with all this extra work you've taken on."

"I'm stronger than I look," she tells him and turns to share a smile, but he's gone. Stopping abruptly, she looks around the room hoping to spot him in the shadows. "Please don't leave." But a resounding silence is her only reply. *I'll play every day in the hope that you'll come back to me.*

Feeling suddenly exhausted, Caroline goes up to her room and falls asleep on her bed. Her dreams are of Travis and cause her to cry out.

I don't want you to leave! In her dream he doesn't leave, he holds her and loves her the way a woman in love needs to be held and loved. His hands explore her body, his soft lips follow tasting her like a starving man at an all you can eat buffet. When he kisses her, there is a depth and passion she has never known before. *Travis! I need you, Travis!*

Listening, just feet away, Travis Lovett is a man tormented. He can hear her dreamy passion, knows that she is dreaming of him. "But how can she love half a man," he growls and heads back up to his self-imposed prison. Yet he felt it, too. That day when she touched his cheek, he'd felt her right in the depths of his soul. For a brief moment he had known peace, until he'd pulled away from her, sure that she would be repulsed by what she had seen.

But what he'd seen in her eyes as her tears fell just before the lift door closed hadn't been fear or revulsion, and he didn't think it had been pity. Then what? *You're a fool even to think a woman like that could ever love you. Stay away! Just stay away or face the pain of rejection for sure!*

When Caroline awakes, she doesn't feel rested. Rather she feels exhausted and needy, lost and alone. *Why didn't you stay? I only wanted you near me.*

Not feeling like food, she continues to organise the charity benefit and puts together an idea for a poster. Having spoken to her dad, she now has confirmation of all the big names she can use to promote the event. After doing a bit of ringing round, Caroline makes an appointment with a printer for later that afternoon. It sounds promising – after some persuasion, they have offered to talk to her about sharing the cost if they get a mention on the poster for their donation.

Taking a walk in the rear hotel gardens, Caroline sits on a bench in the shade of a tree and looks up towards the penthouse. *Are you up there? Are you watching me right now? I hope you are then you'll see how sad you're making me. Why won't you let me love you – surely you felt it too! Can love really be this one sided?*

Getting up to walk again, she strolls over to a small pond. Without embarrassment she laughs out loud, the thought of Catherine's reaction to Charlie, Logan's tame Koi Carp, forming unbidden in her mind's eye. *Oh, Catherine, I'm so very glad we found each other.*

With that thought, she remembers the librarian. Erin Vandivier, she thinks Catherine called her. Apparently, she had been her mother's best friend. *So what could she know that she wasn't telling,* Caroline muses, *and what reason would she have to hide anything now. After all, Sara Colson is dead – what harm can her secret do anyone now?*

Looking back up at the penthouse, she thinks of Travis and his uncanny ability to know everything that is going on around him. *Would he know about mum? Has he lived here that long?*

As Caroline looks up, Travis can see her beautiful smile. He knows she can't see him, but still he stands to one side of the window just in case. He is listening to one of her many concert recordings he has always enjoyed. Only now, he listens to them with an intimate pleasure, picturing the rapture on Caroline's face every time she loses herself in a piece of music.

He has watched her every day since her arrival at The Lovett Hotel. More than happy to allow her the use of the grand piano in the lounge, he has made a point of being present at every one of her practice sessions. And he has seen her with a man; a local named Ben Sharmann. Jealousy is not an emotion Travis usually indulges in, but having seen them together, seen them holding each other in a lovers embrace, he has wished like never before that he was in another man's shoes.

Watching Caroline sit on a bench near the fish pond, he wonders about her relationship with Ben. *Are they lovers? According to the society gossip rags, she had been engaged to Clive Attenborough until very recently. Those same gossip rags had reported the couples break up after a string of affairs had come to light. Mr Attenborough had tried to deny his infidelity, but a bevy of young women had come forward to sell their stories.*

How very foolish men can be! To have held a woman like Caroline, to have owned her heart only to throw it away is stupidity beyond belief.

For the next three days Caroline practices at the piano religiously, even playing for longer than usual in the hope that Travis will show. In the hope that he is at least listening she indulges in a one sided conversation.

"I finalised the posters for the benefit," she tells the empty room. "The printer even asked for volunteers to go poster sticking and a couple actually said they would." For a moment Caroline falls silent and concentrates on her playing. "I adore playing this piece," she smiles and lifts her face to the heavens as she continues. "It should have words, don't you think - hence its name, 'A Song Without Words'. When I wrote it I imagined a sweet voice that could reach notes that only angels might sing." Again,

Caroline falls silent abandoning herself to her music and her imagination.

When she finishes playing she is met with yet more silence. Turning, Caroline looks around the room and realises that not one member of hotel staff is present – then she realises that she hadn't noticed anyone yesterday or the day before. Has Travis forbidden his staff to be present during her practice sessions; if so, why?

Are you giving me privacy to enable me to concentrate fully on my playing – or are you keeping me to yourself? Interesting!

"I wish you would at least talk to me, Travis." Her voice is full of sadness and her blue eyes go round and wide as she searches the shadows for him. "Would it really be so bad to have someone care about you? I would never hurt you, Travis – I've had my heart broken, I would never inflict that pain on anyone else. Never!"

After yet another night of fitful sleep, Caroline decides that part of her problem is the guilt she feels about her relationship with Ben. It had started because she was angry and insecure, needing to take back control and hurting herself and possibly Ben, in the process.

Walking in to the address Catherine has given her, Caroline is seriously impressed by the upgrade in the business accommodations. A small reception area houses a desk and a young woman behind it. She is busy tapping away on a word processor then turns to answer the phone just as Caroline makes her approach.

"Just one moment please," the receptionist presses a button on the small switchboard and puts the call on hold. "I have some letters ready for you to sign, Ms Colson," she tells Caroline obviously mistaking her for Catherine. Then, thrusting a small pile of papers towards her, the receptionist continues, "I've also taken details of two more enquiries asking for you to do a security review as soon as possible – I've put those on top for you to look at." Not waiting for a reply, the young woman picks the call back up on the switchboard and says, "Sorry to have kept you waiting, how may I help you?"

A small passageway to the left of the receptionist's desk appears to lead back to a suite of offices and a modest kitchen. Standing back from sight, Caroline listens as Ben talks and laughs with an unfamiliar female. *The new staff?* Caroline wonders and moves forward cautiously.

The woman sounds as computer savvy as Ben, and he is clearly impressed and more than a little smitten if his goofy grin is anything to go by. Taking a deep breath, Caroline steps in to the kitchen and catches Ben off guard.

"Caroline!" Ben jumps guiltily and stammers over his introductions. "Err...Emma, this is Catherine's sister...Caroline – Caroline, this is Emma one of two new employees who are already worth their weight in gold."

"Wow," Emma thrusts a hand towards Caroline, "I heard Catherine had a twin sister but I never dreamed you'd be so alike. I'm pleased to meet you."

"I'm pleased to meet you too, Emma." Then, looking towards Ben, she smiles, "I'm very pleased to meet you, too. Haven't seen you around for a whi e, Ben?"

Blushing and fumbling to pick up some paperwork from the worktop, Ben steers her out of the kitchen and in to his office. "Oh hell, Caroline, I'm sorry..."

"Ben," putting a quieting finger to his lips, Caroline grins impishly, "I should tell you that I'm broken hearted and make you squirm, but I'm not. And you and Emma look like you're getting on like a house on fire – am I right?"

He still looks unsure and more than a little guilty when he asks, "You're not mad – I mean you really do, do casual?"

Caroline can't help but laugh while Ben just looks stunned. "No, Ben, I'm not mad, and no, I don't do casual either."

Sitting down behind his desk, Ben looks confused and wary. "I don't get it. You were the one who told me that casual was what you wanted, now you say you don't do casual, which is it?"

"When I met you I was hurt and angry," Caroline tells Ben taking a seat opposite him. "I just wanted to take some control back in my life. But I didn't want to be alone. I suppose I needed an intimate friend and you were there for me, just don't feel guilty because it's time to move on."

"Well," Ben says on a sigh of relief, "I can honestly say it was a pleasure being there for you. But I'm glad that you don't do casual, I never really thought you did."

They both stand and, rounding the desk, hug each other with renewed friendship. "Is Catherine around?" Caroline asks as she moves to open the office door.

"She is, but she's got our other new starter, David, with her. Why don't I ring through and let her know you're here?" he offers when Caroline frowns.

"No, no, don't disturb her," she shakes her head and starts walking back toward reception. "I dropped in on the off chance, but I'd appreciate it if you'd let her know I was here, and give her these," Caroline smiles and hands Ben the paperwork the receptionist had given her, "it appears I completely fooled your receptionist."

Stepping back out into the sunshine, Caroline feels like a weight has been lifted off her shoulders.

Now what? I was hoping to ask Catherine if she'd found anything more out about mum, or about Erin Vandivier. Continuing to walk to her car, she contemplates the librarian. *What's to stop me visiting the library on my own? I can wheedle information as well as anyone else. I might even get more out of her on my own.*

The old library looks dull and cold in the shadow the high sun casts over it. Moving to the entrance, Caroline hesitates and straightens her spine as if readying for battle. The temperature drops markedly when she enters the foyer and she gives her bare arms a rub.

A crowd of children sit cross legged on the floor in the far left hand corner of an open reading area. The tables and chairs have been moved to one side and an adult is sat at the front of the group reading a story.

"Oooo," the children groan together, and then giggle when the storyteller makes a sudden growling noise that causes them all to jump.

Caroline smiles widely, remembering such happy times when she had been a girl – then frowns wondering if Catherine had ever known such innocent pleasures. *I should have been there with you; we should have been laughing together. Now I'm going to find out why we weren't!*

Erin Vandivier can see trouble coming at fifty paces – she raised a son who brought trouble home with him on a regular basis. Now she watches it walking, no striding towards her.

"Ms Thornton, how nice to see you again," she smiles politely.

"Really? Does that mean you've decided to tell me what went on between my parents before they split up?" Her manner is forthright and demanding.

Blushing and breathing rapidly, Erin's smile quickly disappears. "You have no right coming in here this way," she gasps and tries to walk away.

But Caroline isn't in the mood to spare the woman's feelings; two little girls, twin sisters, were torn apart when they were only two years old, who had given a damn about their feelings?

"No, Ms Vandivier, it is you that has no right." Caroline's voice is cold and unrelenting. "You are holding the secret of a dead woman over the living, and I want to know why?"

"You don't understand," Erin turns troubled eyes to Caroline. "I gave your mother my word that no matter what, I would never speak of it."

"Do you think my mother ever envisaged Catherine and I finding each other?" Caroline demands quietly. "And would she have wanted her daughters to feel bereft and abandoned with no explanation?"

"I…I…" Erin rubs a hand over troubled eyes. "This doesn't affect just you," she tries to explain. "There are others whose feelings may get hurt with the telling of an old tale. Now where's the sense in that?"

But if Erin had thought to put Caroline off she had another think coming. More than ever, she wanted to know the truth. "Others? What others?"

"I'm not saying any more!" Moving rapidly, Erin hurries through a door marked 'Private'.

Others? Who can she possibly mean? Not dad, he hasn't a clue what went on back then. So, who else could be hurt by her mum's secret?

Driving back to the hotel, Caroline decides that Travis is her next stop. She doesn't care if she has to talk to him through a door, she will ask him what he knows.

The hotel receptionist has the same wary look as Erin Vandivier had when she sees Caroline striding towards her. "Please tell Mr Lovett that Caroline Thornton needs to see him urgently."

Without a word of protest the receptionist picks up the phone and makes the call up to the penthouse. "Yes sir," the receptionist looks up at Caroline then back to the telephone, "Ms Thornton is very insistent." Blushing, the young woman replaces the handset and turns to Caroline. "Mr Lovett said to take the lift, as before, and he will see you now."

"Thank you," and Caroline smiles and gives the receptionist a cheeky wink.

The curtains are closed and the room is in darkness when she emerges from the lift. Looking around, Caroline spots Travis seated on the far side of the room with a vacant chair opposite him and off to his left.

"Come in, Caroline, would you like some refreshments?" he offers politely.

Crossing the room, she indicates the vacant chair and says, "May I?"

Nodding, Travis watches as Caroline takes her seat and frowns down at the carpet. "What's troubling you, Caroline? Is it to do with the benefit?" Then frowns when she silently shakes her head. "If there is anything I can do to help, you know I will – surely that is why you've come to me?"

Getting to her feet, Caroline strides about the room not noticing how Travis has moved back in his seat and turned deeper in to the shadows. "Did you live here about twenty-four years ago? I mean, in Sheriton," she clarifies, "not the hotel."

"I've lived in Sheriton, and the hotel, for all of my life," he tells her, his voice as deep and dark as the shadows he hides in. "What is it you need to know?"

Coming to a stop, Caroline turns to look at Travis. "I need to know why Catherine and I were separated when we were just two years old. I need to know why my mum told the man she supposedly loved, and who absolutely loved her, to leave and allowed him to take me with him as some sort of consolation prize," she demands not realising that her voice has risen to a shout.

"I need to know why Erin Vandivier thinks she has the bloody right to keep the secret of a dead woman when it so badly affects the living." Pacing again, Caroline drags in a shaky breath, "And I need to know who she means by 'others' when she spoke of the harm telling that secret could do." Her voice has grown smaller and without realising it she has retaken her seat. *Others...not more lies and deceit?!*

Standing, Travis moves further back in the room to a small drinks cabinet. Pouring two glasses of wine, he takes care to keep his right side turned away and hands a glass to Caroline then sits back down. "I have wondered if you might ask me about your mother," he tells her. "As it happens, I was friends with Mrs Vandivier's son, Kevin. We are much the same age, though we attended different schools. For some reason we got on really well," and he sounds mystified by the thought. "We were nothing alike," Travis continues. "Kevin was loud and always in trouble, whereas I was quiet and not a little shy." He chuckles to himself, "Perhaps the old saying that opposites attract is true on many levels – it certainly applied to us."

"So you got to know Erin Vandivier?" she asked quietly. *This means you probably knew my mum, too!*

As if guessing her thoughts, Travis recalls an incident he overheard. "I'm not sure that what I remember will help you," he hesitates to give her any more bad news. "I overheard a few conversations; as I'm sure you know Mrs Vandivier and your mother were the best of friends."

Caroline nods, and looks down at her hands, her fingers knotting together.

For endless minutes Travis remains silent, then takes in a fortifying breath and eases it steadily out. "I was at Kevin's house listening to music in the breakfast room. The CD finished playing and I got up to change it," he looks over at Caroline, "that's when I heard your mother and Mrs Vandivier talking. Both women were upset, I couldn't tell which but one of them was crying."

He grimaces and looks away. "I suppose it was the curiosity of youth, but I couldn't help listening harder to what was being said. They talked about going to the police, and then decided it might be for the best if they didn't." He was feeling very uncomfortable about relaying this particular recollection.

Waiting for him to continue, Caroline told him to just spit it out when he didn't. "I need to know, whatever it is – if you don't tell me I'll find out some other way."

He can see that she is determined and decides it would be better coming from him. At least he wouldn't embellish the story as others might. "Someone was raped." Travis hears her gasp and wishes he could offer Caroline some comfort. "I don't know who it was," he tells her quickly, "I just heard them talk about 'the bastard' who did it and what they would like to do to him."

Finishing her wine, Caroline holds her glass out to Travis. "Could I please have another – a large one?"

Taking the glass from her, Travis brings her another larger glass full almost to the top. "I hope you've had lunch?" he asks eyeing Caroline with some concern. *But if she needs a drink as least she hasn't got far to go back to her room.*

Not even bothering to reply, Caroline takes a large gulp of the wine. "Either it happened to my mum," she speculates, "or she believed it was my dad who did it to someone else." *Oh, god. Please don't let that be true. Not my dad! Not a rapist!* "Either way, it's a fucking mess!"

"Shit!" Travis exclaims when Caroline tips the glass up and glugs the rest of the wine down without stopping.

Needless to say, her head starts to spin and the empty glass falls to the floor. Forgetting about staying in the shadows, Travis bolts across the room to catch Caroline before she passes out on the floor. Lifting her into his arms, he holds her close and puts his cheek to hers.

Not having passed out cold, Caroline is aware of Travis holding her and snuggles in to his warmth. "Is this what I have to do to get you to hold me?" she mutters in to his chest. "Typical," she exclaims in disgust, "now I'm too drunk to take advantage of you." And with that her head droops and her eyes close.

"Now what?" Travis frowns down at the woman he has dreamed of holding since she walked in to his hotel. *I can hardly carry her back to her room in the middle of the day. She'll have to stay here until the early hours of the morning then I'll get her back to her room.*

Taking her through to his bedroom, Travis lays her on top of the bed. She doesn't wake, but snuggles in to the pillow with a long sigh.

Watching her, Travis can't help admiring her long shapely legs and how well her figure shows off the short fuchsia sundress. Taking off her shoes he puts them at the side of the bed and leans forward to stroke her short silky hair.

"How lovely you are, my darling Caroline," he tells her and bends to place a tender kiss on her soft lips. *You smell so sweet and tempting, so utterly female. Shall I lay with you, Caroline? Dare I hold you while you sleep and take the memory of you in my arms as my secret treasure?*

Lying down beside Caroline, Travis is content just to be near her. He can see the rise and fall of her chest, her breathing relaxed and even. He'd been a fool to indulge her in so much wine, but he couldn't blame her for needing to dull the pain. So much heartache in so short a time. *I wish I could kiss it all away.*

As if he'd spoken the thought out loud, Caroline calls to him. "Travis, don't go. Why won't you stay with me…just stay," she tells him, her eyes are closed but still a tear manages to fall free.

Holding his hand gently against her cheek, Travis uses his thumb to brush the tear aside. "I'm here, Caroline, sleep now." Moving closer he slides an arm under her head and cradles her against his chest.

Instantly she curls around him, fitting herself against him sighing contentedly. "I love you, Travis." He hardly dares to breathe in case he wakes her and breaks this wonderful spell. Never has Travis known such happiness, and he lies awake to savour every moment of it.

Chapter Eight

"No, no, no," Caroline wakes alone in her room and feels desolate. "I can't take this, Travis! I can't take this anymore!" *You're driving me crazy!*

Getting ready quickly, Caroline leaves the hotel having still not eaten. She hadn't eaten the day before either, but food is the last thing on her mind.

"Catherine…," she sobs in to her mobile when her sister answers, "…I know you're busy, and I really don't mean to intrude…" Caroline has to stop and swallow back the tears. On the other end Catherine is frantic, demanding to know what's wrong. *I need someone to stop me from falling apart!* "I just need some sister time, ok? Can we do that?"

She had meant to drive somewhere, anywhere, but Caroline realises that she is too upset to get behind the wheel. Going back in to the hotel, she makes for the lounge and plays her heart out. She doesn't make her usual effort to talk to Travis, but releases her emotions in to the music. It is dire and chaotic, skipping from one piece to the next, no sense of pleasure involved. Her fingers are flying, her emotions pouring out until she is all but exhausted.

When Catherine walks in, she finds her sister tear soaked. Still playing as if her life depends on it, Caroline is unaware of her surroundings and the terrible state she is in.

"Stop," Catherine calls out, "please, stop!" But Caroline is lost in her pain and the music is her only escape. Walking quickly, Catherine sits and pulls her sister in to her arms and holds on while Caroline's heart breaks and her body racks with desperate sobs. *Dear God help me – I can't bear this pain!*

Listening in the wings Travis is as desperate as Caroline. Wanting to break free of his chains and go to the woman he loves. *Will I ever walk in the light? She thinks she loves me, but could she live with the sight of this every day!* His fingers paw at the uneven scars on his right cheek. *Caroline…would you really want to wake up and see this lying next to you!*

A loud cry of pain echoes from the shadows, as if the building itself is in agony. Catherine gather's Caroline up and guides her to the lift and back to her room. Falling on to her bed she weeps until exhaustion drags her in to sleep.

Once she is sure her sister is fast asleep, Catherine calls Logan and tells him what is going on. "No, no, that's ok," she reassures Logan when he offers to drop everything and come straight over. "Caroline is sleeping and I think she would be embarrassed to wake up and find you here." As much as she would love someone to tell her how to handle this stuff, Catherine knows that she is the only one that can. "I may stay over if you don't mind," she tells Logan and breathes a sigh of relief when he assures her he doesn't. "I'll see how things go, but I wouldn't want to leave her if she's still upset." Her voice lowers and her brows draw together in confusion. "I love her, Logan. When I saw her pain, I felt it right in the heart of me," she tells him. "I don't really understand how that can be, but...Caroline is a part of me...in a way I would never have believed possible."

By the hotel's indoor swimming pool, both girls relax with a fun looking cocktail with ice, coloured stirrers and mini umbrellas. "I can't believe I did that," Caroline exclaims yet again. "I really think it must have been the illness that made me so overwrought and pathetic. I don't believe I have ever fallen apart like that in my life – not even when I found out about Clive, and that messed me up good and proper!"

"For the last time, Caroline, will you just relax," Catherine tells her, "I'm enjoying getting some time together, it wasn't the way I would have wanted it to happen, but I'm good with it. And besides," she looks down at her snazzy swimsuit, "I got a new bathing costume out of it. Though lord knows what Logan would say if he ever saw me in it?" *Not that he ever will!*

It was all the colours of the rainbow in a very artsy, splashy design. Caroline had insisted they get the same, and she hadn't liked the plain navy offering that Catherine had picked out. Boy was she going to have to drag her sister in to the twenty-first century. *In some ways she is just so old fashioned. Is that something she learned from mum, I wonder?*

"Come on sis'," Caroline stands up and holds a hand out to help Catherine up off her lounger, "I want a chance to beat you. You only won by the skin of your teeth the last time."

Despite her reluctance, Caroline drags Catherine to the end of the pool and before she can ready herself for the race dives in leaving her sister gaping after her.

"That's cheating," Catherine calls out, and dives in with a determined competitiveness that has her catching up with Caroline in no time.

Their fingers touch the wall together and a nearby young boy shouts, "Draw," and both girls laugh.

Pushing the hair back from her eyes, Catherine looks at Caroline's too thin frame and again her concern grows. "I'm starved," she declares when her sister joins her back at the loungers. "What do you say to taking a shower in your room and getting a meal in the restaurant here?"

Caroline eyes Catherine suspiciously. "Are you taking care of me little sis?" she asks, her forehead creasing and eyes narrowing.

Shaking her head and pulling the loaned hotel dressing-gown around her, Catherine picks up her bag with Caroline scowling at her side. "Doesn't swimming make you hungry? It does it to me every time."

Entering the lift, both girls look at their reflection in the rear wall mirror. "Christ, it still shocks me," Caroline exclaims, looking from her reflection to Catherine's. "Have you gotten used to it yet?"

Knowing what she means, Catherine shakes her head as she too looks at her own reflection and then Caroline's. "Not in the least. It hits me every time I see you. What do you think dad will think when he sees us together?"

Glad that Catherine doesn't seem to balk anymore when she mentions their dad, Caroline grins mischievously. "You know, we could really have some fun with that. When we dress the same and do our hair and make-up the same, we look identical. I don't believe he would ever tell us apart!"

"I'm not so sure," Catherine's grin was more reserved. "After all, Logan did and we went the whole hog that day."

Stepping in to Caroline's suite, the girls move companionably. As if they have done it all their lives, they move around each other with ease, one seeming to know what the other was going to do and doing something else to accommodate them. By the end of an hour they have showered and changed, Catherine borrowing some of Caroline's clothes to save her going home to pack some for an overnight stay.

"You look good in that," Caroline smiles admiringly as she walks beside Catherine who is now wearing her fuchsia sun-dress. "Though it feels a bit like giving myself a compliment," and both girls giggle at the absurdity of it.

Entering the dining room, the maître d' greets them and has them seated at one of the more private tables. Picking up the menu, Catherine's eyes go round when she looks at all the lovely food on offer. "What are you having?" she asks Caroline enthusiastically. "I'm so hungry I could eat a steak!"

Frowning at the menu, Caroline chooses a seafood salad. "I don't think I could stomach anything too heavy," she smiles an apology across to her sister.

"Well," Catherine sighs heavily, "that has to be an improvement on what you've been eating since you left us. Perhaps you should come back to stay a bit longer, I'm worried about you, Caroline?"

After giving the waiter their order, Caroline sips a cold glass of water. "I think I managed to get it all out, I'll be fine now."

Looking at her sister intently, Catherine can see how pale and transparent her skin still is. "If you won't come to stay with us, at least be honest and tell me what this morning was all about?"

They lock eyes and Caroline finally nods her assent. "Ok, ok." Taking another sip of water she prepares herself to let it all out. "But I'm telling you, not Logan or anyone else, understand?" When Catherine nods she continues. "I told you about Ben, and that part was true," she states firmly, "but I didn't tell you everything. I'm in love," she states simply, and waits for Catherine to voice her disapproval.

"But...who – please don't tell me it's Clive again, not after everything he put you through?"

"No...no it's not Clive," she confirms hesitantly. "Look, I met someone wonderful and I know it sounds crazy...," her eyes plead for understanding; "...but I know I love him. I know with everything inside me that I'm meant to be with him."

Remembering how drawn she had been to Logan right from the off, Catherine smiles and nods. "Logan and I were pretty much the same. I didn't understand what I was feeling at the time, but I knew I didn't like it when he wasn't with me. He makes me feel...whole," she decides then laughs nervously.

"Well I don't feel whole, and that's the problem," Caroline slumps back in her chair. "He won't let me get close to him. He hides himself away as if he's some sort of leper, it's ridiculous!" she huffs, then folds her arms angrily across her chest in a move that Catherine recognises as one of her own.

"I would love to agree with you and give this pathetic man a piece of my mind," she sympathises, "but I can't do that until you tell me who the dickwad is!"

Caroline's cheeks flush and she sits up abruptly. "Travis is not a dickwad! Even if I don't know what it means it sounds insulting," she scowls disapprovingly at

Catherine. "And he is in no way pathetic. He is kind and considerate…and more man than I ever met before." Her voice trails off in to wistful silence and Catherine watches her physically diminish before her eyes.

"Considerate, you say?" Now it's Catherine's turn to sound aggrieved and not a little angry. "Then explain how he has allowed you to get in to this state," she flicks an indicative hand at her sister. "You look worse now than when you were discharged from the hospital. What gives? I thought you were supposed to be the strong one out of the two of us!"

"Well, it looks like I passed that baton to you," Caroline sighs again, all the fight going out of her.

Their meals arrive, and for a while they eat and say nothing.

Then Catherine gets angry again as she watches her sister take the tiniest bites of food and push the rest around her plate. "Eat, Caroline!" she snaps out. "If you don't clear that plate I'm going to call Logan and we'll both cart you off to his place. At least there Mrs Baines will be able to feed you up!"

"Christ you're a bully," Caroline snaps back. "I wouldn't have thought you had it in you." But she does begin to eat and their silence becomes more companionable as Catherine starts to relax.

"Travis who?" Catherine asks out of the blue. "You didn't tell me his last name – I don't think I know anyone named Travis."

"Travis Lovett," Caroline whispers discretely. "He is the owner of this hotel and lives in its penthouse. Though 'lives' is not really an apt description of his life up there!"

Shocked and appalled, Catherine almost chokes on her food. "Jesus, Caroline, he's not known as 'Loony Lovett' for nothing – the man's off his trolley and now you reckon you're in love with him!"

"That's just mean and malicious gossip!" Caroline frowns angrily at her sister. "What justification is there for it? He doesn't come out in public so how can the public judge him." *People! Damned ignorant moronic people!*

"It comes from people who have worked here over the years," Catherine states firmly. "He's known for going off on one at the staff for no particular reason. He just flips, though I haven't heard of him doing anything physical."

"All rumour and gossip," Caroline wags her fork at her sister. "I would expect better from you – I never dreamed you were so small minded."

"So tell me different," Catherine invites. "What makes you think he isn't a loony-toon?" *And if I'm not convinced you are so coming back with me to Logan's!*

"I've spoken with him, and he listens to me play when I practice in the lounge." Putting her knife and fork on her plate, Caroline picks up her water and sips contemplatively. "I have never seen any sign of instability. His only crime is wanting his privacy and that, I believe, is because he's embarrassed, or self-conscious, I'm not sure which."

"What does he have to be embarrassed about?"

Looking at her sister, Caroline is not sure if she is being deliberately insensitive or actually doesn't know about the injuries to Travis's face. "Did you ever hear about Travis being in an accident or being assaulted?" she asks.

Catherine's stunned face tells her the answer even before she gives her reply. "No. Is that what he told you?"

"He hasn't told me anything," Caroline sighs with regret. "He hides in the shadows or keeps his face turned so that you can't see him properly. But I did," her voice is quiet and full of sorrow, "and I felt his pain so deeply."

"So it's his face that's injured?" Catherine asks.

Caroline nods. "The scars look old so I don't think it was a recent accident," she explains. "But I think they are the reason he won't let me love him."

Not knowing what to say, Catherine stays silent.

"He's very knowledgeable about what goes on in Sheriton," Caroline continues. "In fact, I asked him if he knew anything about our parents' breakup."

"And did he?" Catherine asks eagerly.

But Caroline looks wary and struggles to find the right words. "He did tell me something – I'm just not sure what to make of it."

"Just tell me then we can both figure it out."

Taking a deep breath, Caroline tells Catherine exactly what Travis has told her and reaches across the table to take her sister's hands when they start to shake. "I don't know how we can find out the truth," she observes quietly. "I went to see Erin Vandivier again and she was no help – though she did mention 'others' being affected by the secret she's guarding."

For a long moment, Catherine says nothing, and then she looks at Caroline with steel in her eyes. "I'm going to get my laptop and then we'll see what's what."

"How?"

Lowering her voice to a whisper, Catherine tells her, "By hacking in to police records. If our dad was ever suspected of rape it will be on file even if he wasn't charged." Then, when her eyes fill with tears, she swallows them back determinedly. "If it was mum, maybe that's why her medical records suddenly stopped. Perhaps she went to a different doctor because she was embarrassed, or something," she finishes awkwardly. *Please don't let it be mum!*

"Maybe it wasn't anything to do with either of them," Caroline offers, though she doesn't really believe it. "It could be that the secret is Erin's, that she was the one assaulted."

"Maybe."

The next morning Caroline puts in a couple of hours piano practice. She doesn't try to talk with Travis, but forces herself to concentrate only on her music. She didn't tell Catherine, but their dad is due to arrive today and she plans to pick him up from the airport that afternoon.

Coming to the end of her final piece, Caroline closes the piano lid and sits quietly for a minute. Then she looks around the room, staring in to the shadows and says, "It's up to you now, Travis. I can't force you to let me in to your life, though I want that very much. There are only three days left to the benefit, I'd like you to be my escort, but I suppose we'll just have to see."

Watching her leave, Travis is filled with a tumult of emotions. Need, fear and love are just a few, but love is the greatest of them. He has hidden away from the world for so long; how can he step out of the shadows and in to such a bright light as the benefit will surely be? Yet

Caroline wants him to be with her, doesn't seem to be reluctant in the least to be seen with him. Isn't it her opinion of him that should matter? *If only it were that simple. I've loved before and this face is what I got in return. But this life I lead isn't living; it's a pathetic existence that no man should endure.*

Before driving to the airport to pick up her dad, Caroline calls Logan to prepare the way. "I haven't mentioned anything to Catherine," she tells him, "I didn't want to give her the chance to get all worked up and angry. If we can just get them together, I feel sure everything will work out. I know that's what dad is hoping for."

Logan agrees and tells her that he will do his best to make sure Catherine is home by five and ready for them to visit around six.

On the way to the airport, Caroline mulls over her words to Travis that morning. She has no doubt that he heard her; she could feel his presence with every fibre of her being.

If only I could make him realise that his scars mean nothing to me. I love the man I've seen inside. The man I touched and felt right to the heart of me. And I won't give up, not until he tells me to my face that he doesn't want me!

The airport is humming with activity when she enters. An air of excitement buzzes around her; some people are waiting to travel on their holidays and others, like her, are waiting to greet new arrivals.

Looking at the arrivals board, Caroline can see that her dad's flight is on schedule. It should be about an hour, she estimates, before he lands and gets through baggage and customs. Whether it's down to his Irish vagabond looks, or just that he has a guilty expression, there haven't been many times in their travels that he hasn't been pulled over for a luggage search.

Settling herself down for a bit of a wait, Caroline does some people watching. An airport is a fascinating place, she decides, looking around at the milling crowd. Some people look sad at what she presumes is an impending goodbye - other's look up at the arrivals board and smile broadly, most likely excited by the return of a loved one or a visit from someone special.

Just listening to the people around her, she is able to make out French, German, something Latino and at least a couple of different American drawls. *Yep, a real melting pot of colours cultures and styles.*

"Dad!" Caroline yelps when she spots him striding towards her then jumps up to hug him tightly. "Did you get straight through? You almost never do," she laughs, just happy to see him. They rarely go more than a couple of days without seeing each other normally and she has missed him so much.

"This is different," he tells her, giving a gentle tug on her hair. "It suits you."

He hasn't asked about Catherine, and she knows it's because he's nervous. "I'll take you to the hotel first," she explains, "then, if you're up for it, I'll take you to meet Catherine and Logan."

They get his luggage stowed in the boot of her rental car. Her dad's cases are bigger and heavier than Caroline would have anticipated if she had thought of it at all. *Maybe that's a good sign? Perhaps he's planning an extended stay?*

After driving a couple of miles in silence, Caroline tries to relieve the tension by talking about the benefit. "I've managed to get most of the people you confirmed as either attendees or performers booked in to The Lovett Hotel with a handful going to the nearby Sheriton Hall. It's actually quite swanky, the Lord and Lady of the hall still live there and are apparently very welcoming." *Christ, dad, this is like pulling teeth!*

Tom's stomach is in knots. Since Caroline went off to meet her sister, he has kept himself busy trying not to think too much about what might be going on. He knows it was a rocky start, Caroline told him as much, but things have improved enormously. *So, what will she make of me, I wonder? I'm not even sure I have the right to put her through all of this. Damn it!*

"Will you stop worrying," Caroline tells him as she pulls the car in to the hotel car park, "you're making me nervous." The trip had taken under an hour, but it had seemed much longer to Caroline.

"I'm sorry, darling," and Tom gives his daughter a brief hug and a wide smile as they unload his suitcases, "I suppose it's just a bad case of stage fright – you understand." *And it's getting worse by the minute!*

Having settled her dad in to his suite, Caroline goes to her own rooms and calls Logan. "We're back, I just left my dad unpacking the last of his clothes so we should be with you in about half an hour," she tells him. "Is that ok?"

Logan confirms that Catherine is home and relaxing with a glass of wine, so will hopefully be a little more receptive than if she'd had a stressful day.

"Hell, Logan!" Caroline takes a shaky breath. "My dad is so nervous, and to be honest, so am I. Please tell me you think this is a good idea."

Having confirmed that he is fully behind the plan, Logan goes back to keeping Catherine in a calm good mood.

A moment later, Caroline knocks on her dad's hotel door. "Ready?" she asks when he opens it.

"Not in the least!" he replies, and she can see how pale he is, the worry seeming to weigh heavy on his shoulders.

The drive to Logan's house was even quieter than from the airport. Caroline's stomach is churning horribly, and one look at her dad tells her that he isn't fairing any better.

"It'll be ok," she reaches over to put a hand over his as they pull up at the bottom of Logan's drive. "She's skittish and gets angry because she's scared, but give her time and you'll see that under it all, Catherine is a lovely, sensitive woman who cares a great deal for the people she loves."

But will she ever be able to forgive me for leaving her – let alone love me!

Mrs Baines opens the front door just as they reach it. "Caroline, it's lovely to see you," she smiles a warm welcome to them both. "And you must be Mr Thornton, I'm so glad you came. It will be alright now," she nods with a knowing smile. "It won't be easy, but it will be alright in the end."

Tom doesn't answer, but returns her smile with a nervous one of his own.

"Come on, dad," Caroline encourages, "let's go meet your daughter."

Mrs Baines tells Caroline that Logan and her sister are relaxing in the conservatory, then goes off to finish getting the meal ready.

When Catherine looks up and sees Caroline, she beams and makes to get up, but falters when she sees the man behind her. "Holy fuck!" she gasps in shock, and forgotten images from her childhood flash unbidden in her mind. Shaking her head, she sits back down heavily and both Logan and Caroline fly to her side.

"It's alright," Caroline holds Catherine to her and strokes her hair, "it's only dad. He's come for the benefit and wanted to take the chance to see you."

Logan is holding her hand and feels the tension in it.

"I'm alright," Catherine tells them determinately. When she looks up Catherine sees the nervous man and almost feels sorry for him. Almost! *What the fuck are you doing here? Why, after all these years, do you want to meet me now?* "If you think I'm going to run in to your arms, think again!" she states quietly but with an edge of steel that no one could miss. "But I'm glad you're here for Caroline's sake – she's been working herself half to death with this benefit she started."

She said she's glad I'm here — the reason doesn't matter, it's a start!

"Caroline has told me that you have become great friends…"

Catherine cuts him off coldly. "No, we haven't!" she glares at him coldly. "What we have become is what we should always have been — sisters!"

Nodding his head, Tom moves to one of the comfy seats and sits before he falls. "You're right," he concedes softly. "Looking back, I don't know how Sara talked me in to splitting you up, but it seemed to make sense at the time."

Standing abruptly, Catherine's glare has become white hot. "Don't you dare put the blame on mum! It took both of you to make that decision and you seem to have lived with it easy enough!" *Fuck it!*

Caroline slumps back in her seat, shocked and appalled at what she has started. "Please, Catherine, the past is gone…"

"But not forgotten!" she turns on her sister then sees how frail and upset she looks. "Just look at you…damn it!" Moving over to sit next to Caroline, it is Catherine's turn to tend. "Why did you do this — you're already under enough strain, why heap even more on your plate?"

Putting a hand to Catherine's cheek, Caroline's wan smile is pathetic and weak. "Because family is important. Haven't we been finding that out?"

Frowning, hurt and unsure, Catherine looks deep in to her sister's eyes. "I suppose so. But we're different, you and I, we're connected – you know?"

Nodding, Caroline's smile is filled with the love they have found for each other. "My heart knew you before my head," and she leans forward to put a tender kiss on her twin's forehead. "Be strong, Catherine, and at least try to get to know our dad before you judge him. He's already told me a lot of things I would never have guessed at – let him explain them to you then see how you feel – ok?"

Taking a deep, steadying breath, Catherine turns to her dad. "Sounds fair – just don't try to blame mum for everything. She was there for me when you weren't, and she loved me when you didn't – so lay off!"

Chapter Nine

Chaos appeared to reign on the night of the benefit. Caroline and Catherine had spent most of the day with the hotel staff getting the rooms ready as Caroline wanted them. The wall between the dining room and the lounge was folded back and made one enormous hall. The grand piano was front and centre; just a little way back the tables and chairs had been grouped to get as many as possible in to the hall while allowing safe passage between them.

Both girls had been to visit with Chloe, her brother Kyle and their parents that morning. It had gone well, and had given them renewed vigour for getting the job done.

At Caroline's behest, both girls had gone to a beauty parlour and had enjoyed a couple of hours pampering. At least, Caroline had enjoyed it and Catherine had endured it to please her.

Their hair was trimmed and styled, and their make-up was done in neutral, healthy tones and matched perfectly. The girls in the salon had admired them enviously, and said they'd be watching out for them on the TV.

Now Caroline is alone in her room, nervous and excited in equal measure. Looking at her reflection for the hundredth time, she straightens the already straight bodice of the bronze coloured taffeta dress that she had worn on the night of the birthday party.

A knock at her door lets Caroline know it is time to go down. She wishes, again, that she had heard from Travis, but he is a no show and she has to accept his choice. She can't think of the longer term implications of his decision not to be with her. Caroline has to rely on her training and professionalism to get her through tonight and then they would see.

Her dad holds out his arm and Caroline put hers through it. If only Travis had found the courage to be with her – tonight would have been perfect!

Reaching the bottom of the stairs, Tom is called away by one of the hotel staff needing to confirm a few last minute details. Caroline strolls in to the empty hall, it is quiet and a little eerie, but she knows that soon it will be filled with voices and music and life.

"You look stunning, as usual," a man's voice comments from behind her.

Whirling to face him, Caroline stares in wonder. "Clive! What the hell are you doing here?"

"Not quite the greeting I'd hoped for, darling," and he moves to place a kiss on her cheek, "surely we can do better than that." Then he pulls her in to his arms and kisses her with his old passion.

Stunned and angry, Caroline manages to break away. "What the hell are you playing at?" Eyes blazing electric blue, she stumbles a couple of steps to the side. "Did you honestly come here thinking that I would just fall in to your arms and take you back? Are you completely insane?!"

Looking unfazed by her protests, Clive moves closer and again tries to take her in his arms.

"Take your hands off her!" A deep, commanding voice speaks from the shadows. "Or I will break your worthless neck," Travis promises as he moves forward to stand tall and forbidding beside the piano.

"Butt out," Clive dismisses arrogantly. "The lady and I are engaged."

"No!" Caroline gasps loudly. "You made your choices and now I've made mine," she tells him firmly, and moves to stand beside Travis. "I've met someone who is twice the man you could ever be. Just leave, Clive, and never come back!"

Putting her arm through Travis', Caroline hugs closer to him.

When Clive only smirks and stares, she feels Travis stiffen. "You heard, Attenborough," Travis states stonily, "or would you like me to ask one of my security men to throw you out on your arse. You belong in the gutter after all."

"So…you know who I am," Clive observes with interest.

"I know what a worthless lowlife you are," Travis tells him plainly.

"Well…we'll see about that," but Clive doesn't clarify his meaning before turning to leave the hall.

As soon as he's gone Caroline turns in to Travis and he puts his arms protectively around her. "Don't worry I'll have my security team on alert for him. He won't get near you again."

"Oh, Travis," her arms snake around his waist and hug him tightly, "I don't care about Clive, I'm just so happy that you're here, with me."

"And where else would I be on your big night, might I ask?" His smile was so warm and, dared she hope, loving, when she looked up to see him.

"I love you, Travis, and I'll keep telling you every day until you believe it," she tries to smile but feels her lips tremble and a tear fall from her eyes.

Hesitant, he looks down in to blue guileless eyes. "You are an amazing woman, to be sure," he tells her softly. "Your heart is so open and giving, I was worried he would talk you in to taking him back so I had no choice. When I saw him arrive this afternoon, I decided that it was past time for hiding away."

"Then I'm glad he came," she lay her head on his chest and listened to the hectic beat of his heart. "I began to wonder if you would ever let me in to your life – and I want that so badly."

Sounds of chaos outside the doors tear Caroline and Travis apart. "What the hell's going on?" he growls, taking her hand and striding out the doors.

"M...Mr Travis," the indignant manageress greets him in stunned surprise. "These men just barged their way in – the press, sir, wanting to get in first with the story."

"Gentlemen," he greets them graciously, "if you would step outside you will see an area that has been cordoned off especially for the TV and the press. Please take your places, and then feel free to enter the hotel and partake of the free refreshments on offer, after the celebrity guests have arrived."

"So you've got some big names lined up?" One of the men whipped out his notebook and pen. "Can you give us a heads-up – who are they and will any of them be performing?"

"Gentlemen," Travis said a little firmer, "you have already been given a press release by Ms Thornton. Now, you will either take your places outside or be shown off the premises completely – your choice!"

Needless to say, the men left and joined the other media folk in the specially cordoned off area.

"Now, is there anything you would like me to do?" he asks Caroline. "Are there any last minute arrangements you would like me to chase up?"

Looking over his shoulder, Caroline watches her dad approach with a curious smile on his face. "No, actually, your manageress seems to have everything in hand." Holding her hand out to her dad, she pulls him gently in to the conversation. "But I would like you to meet my dad," and reaches up to give the older man a kiss on the cheek. "Hi dad, this is Travis – Travis, this is Tom Thornton, my dad."

"Pleased to meet you, sir," Travis holds out a hand politely.

"And I you, Travis – but why don't you call me Tom, the sir thing makes me feel old."

Travis nods and smiles agreeably, knowing he is going to like this man. "I'll do that, Tom. Are you happy with the arrangements for this evening?"

"You've accommodated Caroline well," he smiles indulgently at his daughter. "I know she can be demanding when she wants something a certain way, but it's only because she cares – more so in this case, as a child is involved." Laughing when Caroline frowns reprovingly at him, Tom tells her that he has to go. "I need to pick up my date," he waves and makes a speedy escape.

"Date?!" Caroline stares after him, and then looks up at Travis flabbergasted. "He did just say date?" then shakes her head when Travis confirms it. A moment later and her mobile rings, "Hi, Catherine, are you and Logan on your way?" Catherine tells her that Andy, Logan's gardener, is really excited as he is going to wear a suit and drive the Mercedes to drop them off and pick them back up later. "So…you're going to turn up in style. You realise the media will think you're one of the celebrities?" Caroline giggles uproariously when she hears Catherine's un-ladylike reply. "And Catherine, ask Logan if Mrs Baines has said she'll be here – dad said he was going to pick up a date, I can only think it might be Mrs Baines, she's the only woman he's met since coming here?"

In the background, Caroline can hear a conversation between Catherine and Logan – Logan confirms that Mrs Baines is not able to get to the event and that he has no idea who their dad might be bringing.

"Hmm…interesting!" *And vaguely worrying.*

"I believe your press is awaiting an interview – didn't you say that you would speak to them before the guests arrive." Looking at his watch, Travis gives a small grimace. "It's about that time," he tells her, pulling Caroline in to his arms for a last hug. "As reluctant as I am to let you go, your public awaits."

The expected quick peck turns in to a leisurely tasting, which rapidly deepens in to full blown passion.

Panting and flushed with colour, Caroline puts a steadying hand to her heart. "Just…hold that thought," she tells Travis with a lusty smile, and is pleased to see that his face is as flushed as hers feels. "We'll finish this later," she promises before whirling away. *You can bet on it!*

After the interview, Caroline steps back out of the lime-light to greet her guests with Travis at her side. She is amazed by his courage, though he still dips his head so that his long hair covers his scared cheek, and turns his head slightly to one side.

A crowd was gathered outside and they knew, from their frantic cries, which celebrity would be next through the hotel doors.

Then Catherine and Logan arrive, and the flashbulbs go off just as eagerly. "Bloody hell!" Catherine shrieks as she nears her sister. "What the fuck? – don't they know a pleb when they see one?!" Then looking at Travis she says, "So, you're Travis." When Caroline moves to intervene, Catherine holds up a silencing hand. Staring straight in to Travis' blue eyes, she narrows her own and says, "You get one warning – break her heart and you'll have me to deal with!" *And you do not want to deal with me!*

Without another word, or backward glance, Catherine strides off to the concert room.

Caroline looks up horrified at Travis and is surprised to see him smiling. "Now that's a formidable woman," he grins at Caroline and holds a hand out to Logan.

"That's why I love her," Logan returns the grin and shakes Travis' hand, "never a dull moment!"

Following Catherine in to the hall, Logan puts an arm across her shoulders and follows a waiter who guides them to a private table.

"Jesus, who are we expecting?" Catherine asks, looking round the table and counting ten seats.

Logan picks up a couple of name cards, "These four settings are for the Harrington family," he tells her while replacing the cards. "Next to them is Caroline and Travis, you and I, then your dad and a mystery guest," he observes, turning the blank name card over in his hand.

Sitting down, Catherine takes a none too discrete look around the room. Spotting a number of very famous faces she raises her eyebrows and turns to Logan. "Do you think Caroline and her dad actually know all these megastars?"

"It wouldn't surprise me in the least," he tells her, not correcting her reference to 'her dad' instead of just dad. "After all, Caroline is a megastar, too. I'm really looking forward to hearing her play."

The only time Catherine heard her sister play was when she'd had some sort of breakdown, and that had been down-right-scary. She frowns over at the piano and hopes that tonight will help obliterate that terrible memory.

The room fills noisily. People from one table, shouting a greeting to people on another table – others laughing and talking like long lost friends.

"Damn it! I hate things like this – it just seems fake somehow!"

"Hmm, I know what you mean," Logan takes a look around the room. "But it's all in a very good cause, and some of these people have extremely deep pockets."

"Well, let's just hope they splash the cash when it comes to donating. Though they probably didn't get rich by giving money away hand over fist," she reasons reluctantly.

"So, does that mean you'll be putting your hand in your pocket?" Logan asks with one eyebrow raised.

"I'll match any donation you make," she tells him with a satisfied nod when Logan frowns.

"That was very cunning, Ms Colson," he tells her in mock reproval. "But whereas I don't mind parting with my cash, you seem to be averse to it."

"Not in the least," she tells him then waves at Caroline to let her know where they are. "I couldn't care less about money – what I hate is someone thinking its ok to rip me off."

As Caroline walks towards them, Catherine can see she is troubled and frowning. "What's up?" she asks, and casts an accusatory glance at Travis.

"It's dad...he's supposed to be here by now."

"And the problem is...?" Catherine asks.

"The problem is," Caroline sits when Travis holds her chair out for her, "dad is meant to be Compére this evening and the Harrington's will be here any minute."

Looking over Caroline's shoulder, Catherine spots the man in question. "Problem solved, he's here." She takes a casual sip of white wine, and then Catherine sputters and coughs so much she has to turn away with a hand over her mouth.

Caroline looks on wide-eyed, and then turns to see what the problem is. "Dad!" Her jaw drops and her wide eyes go even wider. "What on earth...?"

"I understand you've already met Erin," he introduces the woman at his side. "Erin, this is Travis and Logan – Caroline and Catherine you've already met." Holding her chair out for her, Erin takes her seat next to Logan on his left, with Catherine seated on his right. Opposite Catherine, Caroline sits stunned and silent. On her right, Travis watches with interest as the little intrigue unfolds. Tom sits opposite Erin and on Travis' right and smiles round the group as if nothing out of the ordinary is occurring.

Looking at his watch, Tom stands up. "Right then, let's get started," he declares and moves to the front of the hall and to the microphone. "Good evening everyone," he smiles and waits patiently for the last of the stragglers to take their seats.

"I want to thank each and every one of you for coming to this very special event." Using his outstretched hand to indicate everyone in the audience, he gives a small bow of his head to those on his right, then in the centre and lastly to his left where his party is seated on a front row table. A round of applause follows. "The aim of this evening is to raise awareness of Cerebral Palsy and, just as importantly, to raise money for a very special young lady, Chloe Harrington, to attend the Meyo Clinic for some very specialised treatment and therapies." Another round of applause follows.

"Now, ladies and gentlemen, if you take a look around you I'm sure you will recognise quite a few famous faces." People turn in their seats, even the celebrities, to see who is sitting among them. "These wonderful performers, my daughter, Caroline Thornton among them, have come here tonight, at their own cost, to help raise as much money as possible." A rumble of conversation rolls around the room. "We are aiming, not only to fund the Harrington family's trip to the Meyo Clinic, but also to set up an on-going children's charity that will help families with similar needs." This time the applause is enthusiastic and prolonged.

"What we need from you," Tom takes the time to slowly look from one side of the room across to the other, "is lots of dosh!" A roar of good natured laughter breaks out. "This is to be a very unusual auction," he tells them with a big smile and a comic waggle of his eyebrows. "You pledge us as much money as you can, and we give you...absolutely nothing." The audience laugh in confusion and anticipation of the punch line.

"Nothing, that is, except for the memory of your favourite celebrity performing any song you choose, or doing a stand-up comedy spot or, playing the music of your choice." A rumble of approval follows. "First up, will be my daughter, Caroline Thornton, ladies and gentlemen," and he holds his hand out in her direction as Caroline stands and moves forward to the front of the room.

Catherine applauds more enthusiastically than anyone else in the room, and beams with pride.

Tom kisses both of Caroline's cheeks as she takes her place at his side. "Now, who will start the bidding – the highest bidder gets to choose what Caroline will play, don't forget."

The first bid is £1,000 and is quickly followed by another for £2,000. With some encouragement from Tom, the final bid is £12,000 and the music of choice is Rachmaninoff's piano concerto no.3.

Caroline thanks the audience, and particularly the final bidder for their generosity, then takes her seat at the piano. Closing her eyes, and taking a deep cleansing breath, Caroline prepares to play one of the most technically challenging classical piano concertos.

The hum of hushed conversations falls silent as Caroline exhibits her extraordinary talents. Fingers flying across the keys, her heart in every note, she enthrals all who listen and receives a standing ovation at the end.

Caroline takes a bow and walks back to her table. The audience re-seat themselves, except for Catherine. As Caroline nears she wraps her sister in a huge hug and has to swallow back a lump of tears. "I've never heard anything so wonderful. Mum would have been so proud."

Caroline returns the hug and she too has to swallow back her tears.

During the next performance, Tom gets a signal and goes out to the hotel reception to welcome the Harrington family. "Gail, Steve," he clasps their hands in turn with both of his, "I'm glad you made it." Then turning to Kyle, Chloe's almost five year old brother, he offers his hand and Kyle giggles as he shakes it. "Good man," he comments and gives Kyle a wink. "Now then." Crouching down so that he is at eye level with Chloe, Tom smiles and points to his cheek. "Do I get another kiss?" he asks playfully, and then laughs when three year old Chloe rocks back and forth excitedly in her wheelchair and gives a high pitched squeal. Leaning forward, Tom offers his cheek to Chloe and she does her best to give him a kiss. Taking her hand he gives it a kiss in return and receives another excited squeal from Chloe.

Having visited the Harrington's that afternoon with Erin; Tom only has to give them a brief reminder of the proceedings. "We've left a wide enough isle down the centre of the hall to allow for Chloe's wheelchair," he tells Gail and Steve Harrington. "We have a front row table so you'll have no problems seeing what's going on," he smiles at Chloe and Kyle.

"Before we go in," Steve speaks up quickly, "Gail and I want you to know how grateful we are for all your help – and Caroline's, of course." His smile is strained as the months of worry and tension make themselves known. "We can't thank you, and all the kind people that have come here tonight, enough." At his side, Gail is nodding in agreement.

When the hall doors open and Chloe is taken in with her brother and parents at her side, the room at first falls silent then erupts with a huge round of applause. Chloe is a little star and her lovely smile is wide and bright on her excited, beautiful face.

Chapter Ten

It is the early hours of the morning by the time Caroline and Travis make it up to his penthouse.

"You must be exhausted," Travis holds Caroline to him and savours the pleasure of being alone with her. "I thought they would never stop requesting you to play for them – you're still not strong enough to put yourself through so much."

Smiling up at him, Caroline can see the concern in his eyes. "I had you with me, which gave me all the strength I needed." Her hand slides up to the back of his neck and pulls gently until his lips are within reach. Staring straight in to his eyes, she doesn't waver, "I want you, Travis," and closes the small gap with slow deliberation.

What starts out as a tender, sweet joining of mouths soon becomes a desperate mating of passions that have met their perfect match. Caroline's hands are twined in his hair, her body pressed intimately in to him, and Travis' heart is beating fit to burst with a love and need the like of which he has never known.

"Caroline, stop," he begs, worried that she will come to regret this moment.

"Never!" Her hands have been busily removing his clothes and are now exploring the exquisite body they have uncovered. Dropping to her knees she pleasures him eagerly and delights in the guttural roar she draws from him.

When he pulls back from her, Caroline sighs lustily.

"Slow down, Caroline." Travis pulls her in to his arms and holds her there while his mouth explores her face and neck and his nimble fingers unzip her gown.

When she helps him to shrug it down her body, he is surprised by how little she is wearing beneath it. "So beautiful…," one very gentle hand caresses her breast while his lips take in and savour the nipple of the other, "…such a heavenly body and a wonderful gift."

Amazed at how his slow gentleness is arousing her, Caroline feels her body tightening as her skin tingles beneath his touch.

"Come to bed, Caroline," he croons quietly, "where I can love you the way you deserve."

Her breathing is uneven in anticipation of what is to come. To be with him, to lay with Travis in his bed, where she has longed to be night after night, is like a dream that she doesn't want to wake up from.

His bedroom is very male, strong colours and no ornaments or photo-frames. And she can smell him here, his scent is all around her and driving her wild with need.

With unladylike haste, Caroline climbs in to his bed and holds a hand out to beckon Travis to her. "I need you, Travis, as I've never needed a man before – please come to bed."

Sitting on the edge of it, looking at the beautiful woman who is calling to him, Travis feels like he must be dreaming.

"I want to look at you, and remember you here with me," he tells her, his voice filled with the wonder of the moment. Taking her outstretched hand he moves over her and his long hair falls about his face.

"Don't hide from me, my love," she tells him, and moves a hand to cup his ravaged cheek. "I love every part of you, just you, and the man I know you to be inside."

Lowering his face he moves to kiss her generous mouth, lingering to taste the sweetness of her.

Trailing his lips down her throat and across her collar bone, Travis begins an exploration that drives Caroline mad with longing.

He wants to taste, savour and remember every inch of her body, so that when he wakes up alone and the dream is gone, she will remain in his mind's eye forever perfect.

But when Travis wakes in the morning, not only is Caroline still in his bed she is wrapped around him like a second skin.

Barely moving, he watches her sleep, her face tipped up and so beautiful. *If I'm dreaming I never want to wake. This woman, this moment, this soul deep love – can it be real?*

Suddenly Caroline stretches like a cat against him and Travis holds his breath. It isn't dark in his room now, he had been careful last evening to keep his face turned away or well covered; now there would be no hiding place.

Moving to lay full length atop him, Caroline basks in the feel of Travis beneath her. "Good morning, my love." Breathing in the scent of him is so intoxicating. "You smell so good," she tells him and lifts her head to smile up at him. But Travis looks troubled and has his head is turned away from her.

"No, my love, you will never hide again," she tells him. "Not from your staff, from the world, and especially not from me – I love you."

Gently, cupping his cheek, Caroline turns him to face her and smiles with delight and a love so bright Travis can't help but believe her.

"You have turned my world upside down," he tells her, sounding bemused but delighted. "I have never dared dream of such happiness as I believed it beyond me," Travis tells her honestly. "But your heart is so full and generous; I only hope I won't disappoint you in the light of day."

His humble plea is heart-breaking for Caroline - this big strong man, so insecure and afraid to hope for love. "You won't disappoint me as long as you love me," she tells him firmly and moves to sit astride him. "You…are…gorgeous," and she kisses him between each word, drawing a reluctant smile. "I'm only afraid that once the female population gets an eyeful of you I'll be fighting off the competition."

He knows she is joking, but Travis also knows the nightmare she suffered in her relationship with Clive Attenborough. "I would never betray you, Caroline." Reaching up he draws gentle fingers down her soft pale cheek. "I only want to love and care for you."

This time their lovemaking is slow, gentle and reverent. Their hands and mouths move not to take, but to give with every touch.

Love, the greatest aphrodisiac, drives them to heights of pleasure that are beyond the understanding of those that haven't been there.

When Travis pushes in to her, Caroline is transported to another plane – one where love and trust equal happiness and tremendous joy.

A tear escapes her eyes, but she feels no sorrow – only a sense of coming home, of finding her place in this wonderful man's arms.

Moving together, their bodies joined as inextricably as their hearts, their release is profound and intensely satisfying.

Two minds thinking alike, their voices whisper in unison. "I love you."

Her piano practice is a joy. All her love and happiness flow out and in to her music. So involved is she, that Caroline doesn't notice someone enter the room. Moving slowly, quietly, he stands to the side and back of her right shoulder.

Finishing the piece, Caroline straightens her spine, stretches out her arms and fingers then prepares to play some more.

"Always so dedicated."

"Clive!" Spinning round to see him, Caroline is startled by his sudden presence.

"The one and only," he smiles. "I couldn't just leave with things the way they were." His voice is soft and regretful. "I let you slip through my fingers - I was a fool."

"Don't, Clive," Caroline pleads, feeling guilty for her own happiness when Clive appears to be suffering. After all, she did love him once. "What's past is behind us – we've both moved on."

Heaving a heavy sigh, Clive moves to stand at the edge of the piano to regard her. "I wish I could agree with that," and he gives her a rueful smile. "Unfortunately, I seem to be a classic case of not knowing what you've got until it's gone – I love you, Caroline, with all my heart." Pushing his hands back through his hair, his face looks strained. "I was hoping you would give me a second chance…"

Caroline is dumbstruck. He really appears to be sincere. He has a defeated look about him and Caroline can't help the thawing of her anger towards him. "I daresay, if I hadn't met Travis, that might have been a possibility – but Travis is my life, now."

"I always thought your music was your life," Clive muses with some of his old rancour. "You certainly paid it more attention than you did me."

"And you're saying that's why you had other women?" she asks, astounded.

"Well, it does get lonely just sitting around waiting for you to come home from yet another tour," he pouts sullenly.

"But, Clive, you have your own music career to work on," she reasons. "You have such talent, why would you not make the most of it?"

His laugh was deprecating and bitter. "Oh it's alright for some," he sneers, "you had a gift given to you and you've always exploited it well. But some of us have to work at it and haven't had the same lucky breaks."

As Caroline listens to him, she realises that Clive had always been envious and, yes, even jealous of her success. "I may have a natural aptitude for the piano," she tells him with more steel in her voice, "but I do work hard to improve my playing." Her blue eyes harden and her soft heart remembers the pain he put her through. "Instead of feeling sorry for yourself, perhaps you should be working harder at your musical rather than your sexual performance."

"You think you're so superior," he bites out angrily. But Caroline just turns back to her piano and begins to practice, hoping that Clive will take the hint and leave. "Bitch!" he spits out then slams the lid down hard on her fingers.

Caroline's pained scream is followed immediately by an angry roar emerging from the shadows. Clive actually looks scared by what he's done, and backs off when he sees Travis striding towards him.

The door to the lounge opens and a number of people enter, blocking Clive's escape.

"Stop him," Travis roars, and watches as two security men take hold of Clive. "Call the police; I want that man arrested for assault on Ms Thornton!" Turning back to Caroline, Travis is horrified to see her holding her shaking hands out in front of her, tears streaming down her terrified face.

"It'll be alright, Caroline," he soothes, but her fingers are already swelling and have an angry red line developing across them. "I'll get you straight to the hospital and we'll get the best specialists money can buy to look after you."

The hotel manageress sidles up to take stock of the situation and starts barking orders to her aid. "I want you to contact Mr Thornton in his suite, but do not apprise him of the situation on the telephone – you'll panic the poor man," she states firmly. "Just tell him that he is needed in the hotel lounge as a matter of urgency."

Her aid leaves to do her bidding and the manageress turns worried eyes to her boss. "Mr Travis," she addresses him in her usual casual but respectful manner he prefers. "Should we call an ambulance, or had you something else in mind?"

"Caroline?" When she looks up at him, Travis feels his heart clench with pain. "I'm going to arrange for the local doctor to come and stabilise your fingers, then, with your permission I'll contact a friend of mine who runs the local airfield for light aircraft. I want to charter one to take us to the Royal Lincoln, it has some of the top Neuro and Orthopaedic surgeons."

Nodding, Caroline cannot speak with the pain and shock of her injuries.

Then she hears her dad's voice, worried and questioning the staff. "What's happened, is it Caroline...is she ill?"

When he reaches the piano and sees her hands, Tom falls to his knees in front of her, wanting to hold and comfort his daughter, but not daring to move any nearer. "Oh, baby, how did this happen?"

But Caroline just shakes her head and continues to sob quiet unrelenting tears.

Travis fills him in on what he heard and his plans for transporting Caroline to the Royal Lincoln Hospital. "That sounds like a damned good plan," Tom pats Travis on his shoulder. "Thank God you were nearby when it happened!"

"I'm not leaving you," Travis tells Caroline, who looks scared when he stands to make the arrangements. "Your father will stay with you while I speak to Jasper, and get the doctor."

"C..Catherine…," she manages to gasp between sobs.

"I'll call her too," he assures her. "I'm sure Jasper will have a plane big enough to take us all. Ok?"

When she nods, Travis hurries off to get everything underway. The manageress follows behind him, offering to contact Ms Colson and the local doctor while he sorts out the plane.

"No! Oh, no!" Catherine cries out and slumps down in a chair when she hears the news.

Logan and Mrs Baines both come running to the sitting room and find Catherine in tears, having just replaced the receiver.

"What is it, Catherine? What the hell's happened?" Logan demands to know.

"It's Caroline," and when she looks up her eyes are filled with pain and Logan knows it has to be bad. Moving to crouch in front of her he takes her hands to offer some comfort. "Clive Attenborough is under arrest for assaulting her."

"At least they got the bastard!" Logan's oath is guttural and full of loathing. "How badly is she hurt?"

"It's her hands," her lips tremble piteously, "he deliberately hurt her hands by slamming the piano lid down on them while she was practicing." *Her beautiful hands! How will she live if she can never play again!*

Leaning forward, Catherine puts her arms around Logan's neck and holds tight while her heart breaks.

After the doctor has stabilised Caroline's fingers he gives her a small dose of Morphine for the pain. "I'm afraid that's all I dare give you," he tells Caroline. "It's possible that they will want to get you x-rayed and then in to surgery. I don't want you to eat or drink anything before you see the specialist." He looks up at Travis as he returns after carrying out his tasks. "I understand you plan to fly Ms Thornton to the Royal Lincoln?" And when Travis nods he continues, "Very good. As soon as possible please, Mr Lovett, that Morphine won't keep her comfortable for long, but I daren't give her anymore."

Turning to Caroline, Travis places a hand on her shoulder then crouches to stroke her hair. "Catherine and Logan are on their way," he smiles sadly. "Logan knows Jasper and where the airfield is, he's going to meet us there."

Nodding, Caroline swallows a sob. "Thank you, Travis."

She actually manages a tremulous smile, but he knows it is only the Morphine that has calmed her.

"Do you want me to carry you?" he asks, and moves to pick her up when she nods, childlike. "Lift your arms and put one around my neck," he tells Caroline then lifts her carefully. "You weigh nothing at all," he frowns down, hating her frailty, "we'll put that right with a good holiday when this is all over. Just you and me in the sun," he promises and gets another tremulous smile before Caroline lays her head on his shoulder.

The flight is thankfully short and uneventful. Catherine hasn't left her sister's side, even sitting close to her dad in order to sit as close to Caroline as the seating will allow.

When they arrive at the hospital a host of staff are already on standby and whisk Caroline away with Travis hot on their heels.

The rest are shown to a private waiting room. "It seems Travis has paid for the best," Catherine states woodenly, trying not to give in to useless tears. "We have all the comforts of home," and points to a machine for making every kind of hot drink imaginable using expensive looking sachets that slot in to make it up fresh. *A cup of tea, the English answer to every crisis. Fuck! Fuck! Fuck!*

Chapter Eleven

Travis arranged accommodations for everyone at a local hotel. However, as he sits at Caroline's bedside stroking her hair, he knows that neither her dad nor Catherine have left the waiting room.

They are kindly giving him some privacy. "You sleep well, my love. The surgeons were pleased with how things looked," he tells her unmoving form. "They think you'll need some physio' once you've started to heal properly. No doubt it'll be hard work, but you're used to that already."

Laying his head on the bed next to Caroline's, Travis tries to tell himself that she will wake up and all will be right with the world again. But he is afraid for her. The surgeons were not entirely sure that they had been able to repair the nerve damage to her hands and warned it could take up to a year to recover all the movement even if they were successful.

Catherine walks in to Caroline's hospital room to find Travis fast asleep, his head resting on the bed near to Caroline's. *So, you found love – but the tragedy wasn't far behind. Are the Colson women never to find true happiness?*

Drawing up a chair, Catherine sits and lays her head on the opposite side of the bed to Travis. "You need to wake up, soon," she whispers softly. "Travis needs you and so do I." Unaware that her voice has woken Travis, Catherine continues, "Now that you've found the right man, life will be wonderful again – I can vouch for that," she insists still whispering softly, "I was so lucky to find Logan, and Travis seems to be made of the same stuff."

Travis is embarrassed that he is listening in on a private conversation, but feels that letting Catherine know that he is awake and listening will only cause more embarrassment.

"I don't know if you get angry, too, when you get frightened or hurt, but Logan's really good at ignoring me and letting me get it all out." Giving a quiet self-deprecating laugh, Catherine says, "I don't know why he puts up with me, I'm sure he could have his pick of much nicer women. I bet if he'd met you first you would have been right up his street. You know all about that etiquette shit, but he says he isn't bothered about all that, just tells me what I need to know when I need to know it." She's rambling now, talking about anything so as not to sit in terrifying silence.

"Mum would have loved what you did for Chloe. And Kyle loved his birthday present – it was nice the way you made him feel special, too. I bet he loses out like that, everyone fussing over Chloe most of the time."

Falling silent, she reaches out to stroke Caroline's hair. "I love you, sis'," she uses the familiar term that Caroline often does; then slowly falls into a troubled sleep.

After a few minutes of silence and listening to Catherine's breathing shallow out, Travis sits up and regards the two identical women.

On the surface they are identical, he muses, but he feels he would know his Caroline anywhere.

When Caroline smiles or laughs she has a brightness about her – an air of excitement and love of life that positively shines out of her.

Never more so than when she is playing the piano, he thinks sadly. "I pray the Lord to give you back your gift, my love," and Travis stands to place a kiss on her warm lips. "He brought me you, so there must be miracles left in this world — I ask for just one more and will never ask for anything else."

Sitting back down, Travis is true to his word, and spends the next few hours praying for Caroline.

The time has come for the bandages to be removed, and Caroline is so nervous that she almost asks the specialist to leave them on.

Travis can see her fear and sits close to offer his support. "We are all here for you, Caroline. We will help you to get well."

Nodding to Mr Wallis, her surgeon, Caroline holds out her hands to allow him to remove the dressings.

Slowly, and with great care, he unwinds the bandages on her left hand then removes the dressings beneath. Touching the badly bruised fingers gently, he asks if she has any pain or loss of feeling.

"No, no pain," she is relieved to say, "and I can feel you touching me — that's good, isn't it?"

"So far so good," he smiles reassuringly. "Now, let's look at the other hand."

Following the same procedure, he removes the dressings and gently touches her right hand.

"No pain," she states, "but when you touched my middle and forefinger it didn't feel right." Looking up at the surgeon with worried eyes she asks, "Will that come back – I mean is that due to the injury or the surgery?"

Cautiously Mr Wallis examines her hand again. "It's too soon to say for sure, but either way it may recover with care and time."

Biting down on her lip to stop it trembling, she turns to Catherine and tries to smile. "Well, sis', maybe I could come and work for you?"

Catherine winces at the pathetic attempt at humour and shakes her head. "Not a chance!" and she looks deadly serious and determined. "I've heard you play and it's a God given talent you have, so don't go throwing it away at the first sign of trouble!"

Logan is surprised to hear Catherine's declaration, not realising that she had any religious beliefs.

"Well, for heaven's sake," Caroline sulks, "can't a girl have a pity-party even for one day?"

Mr Wallis chuckles and picks up her notes. "You can have today off, but tomorrow the serious work begins. The Physiotherapist will be up to see you in the morning to begin manipulating your joints –it will be up to you to be vigilant about doing the exercises that he shows you."

With that he leaves Caroline alone with her family. "Great!" she huffs flopping back on her pillows.

"Mrs Baines will love spoiling you," Logan says with a broad smile, "so it isn't all bad."

Travis looks crestfallen but stays quiet.

"Actually, I rather thought I might go home with Travis," Caroline smiles up at him tentatively then beams when he nods and smiles his approval.

When Logan spots Catherine's move to interfere, he gives her a subtle nudge in the ribs and gives the plan his approval, too, thus effectively silencing any protests.

Scowling up at Logan, Catherine rubs her ribs with comic emphasis. "It seems everyone agrees," she gives in ungraciously. Then looks across at Travis, "That means you take responsibility for taking care of her," and jerks a thumb in her sister's direction. "That also means I'll be paying regular visits to see that you do!" *She's my sister after all!*

"You will be most welcome." Travis is careful not to smile in case Catherine thinks he is laughing at her. He has come to realise that her brashness is a cover for her uncertainty. "I will employ a private nurse to ensure your sister's care is the best it can be and will make sure that she rests adequately."

"Not too much," Catherine warns with a concerned frown, "you heard the doctor – she has to do her exercises and eventually will need to get back to practising on the piano."

"If you two have quite finished," Caroline folds her arms across her chest and huffs defiantly, "I might actually have something to say about my care!"

Logan laughs and three sets of eyes turn to look at him askance. "Sorry. Sorry," he repeats when he fails to stem his laughter. "It's just that… I've seen Catherine…do…that exact same thing," he points to Caroline's crossed arms and manages to tame his laughter in to a manly chuckle.

"You are so weird," Catherine shakes her head at Logan.

"Sorry," he says again having finally won control.

"So, when do I get out of here?" Caroline asks hopefully. "I mean, if I'm going to have professional care at home, why stay here?"

As tempting as it is to take her back to the penthouse and have her all to himself, Travis is concerned that Caroline is rushing things. "Mr Wallis mentioned starting your physio tomorrow," he reminds her gently. "Perhaps, when you've become proficient at the necessary exercises, you could practice them at home with the nurse?"

"Yes, good idea," Catherine approves and earns a scowl from her sister. "At least you picked a man with a brain in his head this time and not in his balls like that fucker Clive!"

Logan decides that visiting time is over and moves to give Caroline a parting kiss. "Be a good girl and do as the doctors tell you." Then he gives Catherine an encouraging look and she too moves forward to say goodbye.

"Hang in there, sis'," she hugs Caroline and places a kiss on her cheek. "It seems we have to go," and she frowns curiously at Logan.

Just as they turn to leave, the door to Caroline's room opens and Tom walks in.

"Wow, better late than never!" Catherine throws him a bitter scowl and shakes her head then turns back to Caroline and gives her a last wave.

"Don't worry, dad," Caroline reassures him as he crosses to her bedside, "she doesn't really mean it."

Giving his daughter a kiss, Tom pulls up a chair and sits down. "I'm not so sure." He looks back at the door picturing Catherine's face and the contempt he saw there. "I don't think she'll ever forgive me for leaving – no matter what the reason."

Caroline watches him rub a hand over tired eyes then notices his pallor and his tight expression. "What is it…you look worried to death – what's wrong?"

Pushing his hands back through his long black hair, Tom tries to think of a way to tell Caroline what he has learned about her mother. The information is shocking and he doesn't think now is the right time to tell her.

"I'm just tired," he lies badly, "I didn't get much sleep last night and I feel bad about not being here when you had your bandages off." Thinking to use that thought to distract her, he asks Caroline how it went. "Were they pleased with the outcome? Can you move your fingers alright?"

Caroline knows what he's doing but obliges by showing him her hands. "These two fingers are still a bit numb," she shows him but moves them all with some satisfaction. "Now tell me what's really wrong – and don't give me any more excuses."

Looking at his daughter's determined face, Tom knows that any delaying tactics won't work. "I've been seeing a bit of Erin," he begins nervously.

"Yes, we noticed at the benefit," she tells him. "But what has she got to do with how awful you look?"

Getting to his feet, Tom begins to pace the room. "This is difficult, Caroline, and I'm not sure you're up to hearing what I've learned." He turns to look at her studying her pale face. "You've got enough on your plate; this can wait a while longer."

Not saying a word, Caroline simply continues to look at him expectantly.

Heaving a deep sigh, Tom returns to his seat and bows his head. "It's about your mum."

Caroline actually sits forward then and reaches to place a hand on his arm, but remains silent giving him the time to tell her in his own way.

"You already know that Erin was your mum's best friend. Apparently they confided in each other and trusted in their friendship completely." Tom stops to gather his thoughts. "I can't think of a way to say this other than coming right out with it, so here it is," he warns. "Your mum was raped and fell pregnant and was too ashamed to tell me."

Travis sucks in a shocked breath and watches Caroline take in the dreadful news.

"This is why you let Catherine leave," she states knowingly, a trembling hand covering her lips. "You didn't want to tell her the truth."

Tom closes his eyes and puts his head in his hands. "How can I tell her that what her mother suffered wasn't for the first time? How can I add to her pain like that?

Because it's still there, you can see it every time her mum is mentioned, that awful pain is still there."

She knows he is right but Caroline also knows Catherine has to be told. "I'll tell her," she pats his arm and looks up at Travis for support.

He puts a hand on her shoulder and nods. "I think that would be for the best – she'll take it better coming from you."

He doesn't like to think of the strain this will put Caroline under, but Travis knows she is right in this. *Another stress. Another worry. Another weight on your frail shoulders.*

When her mind begins to clear, Caroline thinks of the baby. "Did she have an abortion or did she lose the baby?" she asks her dad softly.

When he looks up his eyes are wide and full of hurt. "Neither, that's why she made me leave," and he looks bewildered by the thought. "Sara couldn't bear the idea of an abortion, she always did have strong feelings about that," he tells her. "So she carried the baby to full term then gave it up for adoption without telling anyone what had happened – except for Erin, of course," he qualifies dazedly.

Tears begin falling heedless down his cheeks. "Did she think I wouldn't understand or that I would simply stop loving her?" he asks no one in particular. "As if I ever could!" *I never stopped loving you, Sara. Never!*

Caroline tries to stay strong for her dad, but her heart is breaking inside. "Poor mum, she suffered so much — thank heaven she at least had Erin to talk to."

"Yes, that's what I told her, but Erin is feeling guilty about the whole thing though she tried to convince Sara to tell me. But Sara wouldn't hear of it." He gets up and begins moving restlessly round the room.

"Once she'd got me out of the way, Sara began looking for a suitable family to adopt the baby. Someone who could give the child a good and loving home, with enough money to make sure it didn't go without."

"So, Catherine and I…we have a half brother or sister somewhere out there," Caroline can hardly believe what she is thinking.

Her shoulders have slumped and her face is deathly pale. "You need to rest," Travis encourages. "This can all wait until you are strong enough to deal with it. Right now you need to rest," he urges again.

"You're quite right," Tom moves back to her side to give Caroline a brief hug and a kiss. "Get some rest and we'll talk about all this another day."

Chapter Twelve

Caroline looks down at her hands. The deeper bruising is fading now, only to be replaced with multi-coloured blotches.

Crikey!

"Not very pretty now," she tells Travis when he comes to sit beside her. "I didn't know bruises could turn so many colours." Then she smiles the smile Travis loves, the one that tells him she can see something good in any situation. "Actually, they sort of remind me of a tortoise I had as a child," and she looks up with a sparkle in her eyes, "his name was Barney and I swear his shell was just these colours. See," putting her hands side-by-side, Caroline rounds them to look like a tortoise shell and laughs, "Barney."

Heart overflowing, Travis puts an arm across her shoulders and pulls her gently towards him to place a kiss on her upturned face. "I will never tire of seeing your lovely smile – it lights my world and makes it beautiful again."

Putting a hand to his damaged cheek, Caroline's eyes burn brighter than ever with the depth of her love for this wonderful man. "You are beautiful." Leaning forward her kiss is tender, her lips so soft and giving. *How could anyone think differently?*

A cough from the doorway tells them that Shanna, Caroline's live in nurse, is waiting to see her. "Sorry, but it's time for your meds'" she tells Caroline. "If you take them now they'll kick in just nice for when physio arrives."

In the hospital her pain had been so well controlled that Caroline had tried doing without her tablets when she came home. Shanna had tried to talk her out of it, and Caroline soon wished she had listened when she woke in the night her fingers cramping with pain.

Travis had gone to fetch the nurse and had worried over her the rest of the night.

"Hmm, I think Charlie is a secret sadist," and she grimaces at the thought of another session with the physio.

"I thought it was getting easier," Travis frowns, concern written all over him.

"I'm just being a baby," Caroline reassures him. "Charlie is great; he puts up with my whingeing and gets the job done in spite of me."

"When do you think you'll start practicing the piano again?" It's a question Travis has put off asking but her father raised the same concern with him the night before.

Swallowing her tablets, Caroline almost chokes on the milk she is drinking. "Look at these hands," and she thrust the nearest one under his nose, "do they look like they could play Dixie, let alone a decent concerto?" *Bloody hell! Anyone would think I didn't want to play again. Shit!*

Shanna and Travis share a concerned look over the top of Caroline's head as she reaches to put her glass down on a nearby table.

"I'm not criticising, Caroline," he assures her, "I just wondered if you have some kind of plan. You're the expert, after all."

Somewhat mollified, Caroline relaxes back on the settee. "Fine! Well, I don't!" *How can I – I've never been in this situation before. And I'm scared...*

"Isn't Catherine due to arrive soon?" Travis asks to change the subject.

Her smile back in place, Caroline grins up at him. "She is. She wants to meet Charlie – I think Catherine wants to make sure he's doing a good job. You know," she chuckles, "not torturing me."

Both Travis and Shanna join in her laughter, relieved to have broken the tension.

As if on cue, they hear the lift bell that signals its arrival. The door opens and a formidable looking Catherine steps out.

"See!" Caroline laughs and Catherine looks bemused.

"What?" Catherine asks looking down at her lemon and white dress for signs of something wrong.

Caroline gets up to embrace her sister. "Nothing, nothing," she chuckles softly. "I just told them that you were coming to suss out Charlie and then you step off the lift looking like you really mean business."

Her cheeks flush bright red but Catherine stands her ground. "That's because I do," she states firmly. "I didn't like the sound of what you told me. If that fucker is getting his kicks by hurting you I'll be kicking his arse out the door!"

"I vetted him myself," Travis tries to assure her, but Catherine is having none of it.

"Fine, now I'll vet him!" and she stands firm with her arms crossed over her chest.

Putting an arm through Catherine's, Caroline draws her forward and in to the kitchen. "I'm dying for a cup of Lady Grey," she tells her sister and lifts a cup to ask if she wants one.

"Ok, but no sugar, you forgot last time," and Catherine grimaces at the memory.

"Fine, white no sugar coming up."

Sitting at the kitchen table together, Caroline wonders if now is a good time to tell Catherine the news her dad gave her in the hospital. They still have half an hour before Charlie is due.

"Come on, Caroline," Catherine urges, "just spit it out – I can tell when you're holding back on me."

"Ok, you're right," she confirms and takes a sip of her tea before starting. "You remember the day I had my bandages removed, dad was late and you were cross with him?"

Nodding, Catherine's eyes narrow suspiciously. "I remember, he never seems to be in the right place at the right time," she quips sarcastically.

"Well, this time he was," Caroline sighs and closes her eyes. When she opens them Catherine is regarding her sceptically. "He was with Erin, he's been seeing quite a bit of her, apparently."

"And I would be interested in this, why?"

"If I'm going to get through this you need to listen with an open heart," Caroline remonstrates quietly. "Dad is not the bad guy you seem to think he is; it was mum who drove him away."

"So he says," Catherine replies hotly.

"So Erin says," Caroline corrects. "She has finally come clean about mum's secret." Getting up, she starts to make another pot of tea for something to do. "Dad was never accused of rape, and Erin wasn't raped either." She lets the words hang in the air then turns to look at Catherine.

"I knew it," Catherine whispers, then rubs her hands over her eyes as if trying to erase the thoughts in her head. "I've been checking through all kinds of data just trying to find any clue, and the only clue is the missing doctor's notes. The more I thought about it the more I was convinced it was mum who was attacked; I just didn't want it to be true, not again." *Life's a fucking bitch! Christ, mum!*

Coming back to the table with two fresh cups of tea, Caroline puts a hand over Catherine's. "I'm afraid that isn't the whole of it," and she waits for Catherine to look at her. "She fell pregnant, that was the main reason she drove dad away. Although, according to Erin, she was too ashamed to tell dad, or the authorities, what had happened to her."

"And you know all this, how?"

"Partly from dad, that day in the hospital – he told me why he was late." Looking down in to her tea, Caroline hesitates. "I also asked Travis to drive me over to Erin's house. I know I should have asked you to come, too, but I wanted to be sure before I told you anything," she pleads. "You've already been through so much; I couldn't put you through more without being absolutely sure it was true."

Sitting silently sipping her tea, Catherine takes the time to think it all through. "So, mum not only gets raped and loses the man she loves, but also has to go through an abortion on her own." Her voice turns bitter. "Or did Erin go with her and hold her hand. That woman seems to have been involved with everything else!"

"Oh, god, Catherine – I'm just going to say it, because there is no good way to tell you," and Caroline takes a steadying breath then launches in. "There was no abortion, and she didn't miscarry either. Mum had the baby then found a well off couple she thought would give the child a good home and let them adopt it."

Sitting back in her chair, Catherine's mouth opens and closes with several responses that she can't quite make.

"I know," Caroline continues, "it's a startling prospect – a half-brother or sister, about three years younger than us!"

"There's no half about it," Catherine states firmly. "I don't give a shit about their parentage, they're our flesh and blood and we need to find them!" Pushing her tea away from her, she looks Caroline square in the eyes. "There's only one half that I can't, won't," she corrects, "live with, and that's half truths between us – we're either sisters or we're not, but sisters don't hide things from each other!"

Caroline is about to tell her that the world isn't so black and white, and then realises that for Catherine it is. "You're right," she concedes, "I snuck around you with the best of intentions, but if that's the way you want it, that's how it will be from now on."

"Good enough," Catherine lets out a long sigh, not realising that she had been holding her breath. She doesn't want to lose her sister again, but straight is as a die in her world.

"Come on, I'm pretty sure I just heard Charlie arrive – don't give him too hard a time," she pleads when Catherine jumps to her feet.

Tom and Erin are having lunch in the park as it is such a lovely day, and it's only round the corner from the library. "Do you think Caroline has told Catherine yet?" Erin asks, and Tom knows exactly what she is referring to.

"No. If she had I'm sure I would have heard about it by now." Shaking his head sadly, Tom thinks about his troubled daughter with a lot of regret. "Catherine should never have gone in to the foster system," he declares. "If I hadn't listened to those bloody social workers she'd have lived with me and known her sister sooner. The poor kid's been kicked from pillar to post – is it any wonder she's so defensive?"

"You can't keep punishing yourself this way," Erin tells him. "You have both your daughters now; it's the future that matters not the past."

"Hmm," is all he says as he plucks unthinkingly at the grass. "Do you have any idea about the couple that adopted Sara's baby?"

Erin almost drops her sandwich at the sudden and uncomfortable turn in conversation.

"Erin, this is no time for holding back!" he warns sternly. "Do you think Catherine won't ask you the same question when she finds out she has another brother or sister out there? You've seen how fiercely bonded the girls have become – I don't think that's just down to being identical twins," he observes sagely. "Catherine has a strong sense of family now that she knows she has one – it makes me wonder if that's what she wanted most as she was growing up, just to be part of a family."

"Maybe," Erin hedges, "but she hasn't made much effort with you – aren't you just as much her family?"

His laugh is rough and self-deprecating. "Well now, there's a world of difference in my case," he explains. "Caroline was taken from her, her mother was murdered and this new member was given away without any choice. But me," he stabs a finger in his chest, "I walked away and left her behind. And worse – I wasn't there to protect her mum. In Catherine's eyes, there is no greater betrayal."

"But…that's…ridiculous!" Erin splutters taking umbrage on his behalf. "You never would have left if Sara hadn't forced you to. You need to tell her everything and explain your side," she tells him. "How will Catherine ever understand if she doesn't know all the facts?"

Nodding, Tom silently agrees. "The couple, Erin, who were they?"

Alone at last, Caroline and Travis snuggle up on the settee listening to music. "Apart from your concert albums, this is some of my favourite music to listen to in the evenings," he tells her. "Her name is Adrianne Adams and she has the voice of an angel."

Caroline smiles up at him, "Should I be jealous?"

"Never!" and he bends to kiss her. "My heart is yours to do with as you will, lock stock and barrel."

"That's a heady power you're laying at my feet," and Caroline places her hand on the back of his neck to draw him to her.

"It's my heart that is at your feet, but the rest of me is all yours, too," and he closes the small gap between them.

What a man you are, Travis Lovett. You give of yourself so freely yet take so little in return. One day I'll make you see just how much I love you, I don't know how but I will. Promise!

When the kiss deepens Travis tries to pull away but Caroline moves with him. "I need you, Travis," she tells him, her hot breath close to his ear. "I've lain with you night after night and you never touch me." She sounds hurt, but most of all she sounds frustrated.

"That's because I don't want to hurt you," and Travis smoothes her growing fringe back from her eyes.

"But I'm much better," and she flexes her fingers to show him. "See, no pain," then she spoils the effect by wincing. "Ok, not much pain, and I won't even use my hands if that's what you want," she grins wickedly and Travis actually feels his cheeks heat up.

"Caroline, you are impossible," but even he has to laugh when she jiggles her eyebrows suggestively at him. "Ok, let's go to bed but you keep your hands safe and to yourself," he admonishes. Then he pulls her up and into his arms. "Just lay back and let me love you, my darling woman."

As they kiss and Caroline feels the fire building inside of her, she naturally tries to undo his shirt to get to the body she craves beneath. With a low chuckle Travis puts a gentle hand over hers to stop her. "Behave, or we'll just get a good night's sleep," he warns, and laughs out loud when Caroline whips both hands behind her back.

"You first," Caroline says when they are in the bedroom and he reaches out to undress her. "If I can't touch at least I can look," and she cocks a cheeky grin at him.

"Such a demanding woman," he moans playfully as he does her bidding. "Now…," but instead of continuing the thought Travis shows her instead. Her head falls back to allow his lips to explore her neck, then she groans loudly when his mouth, tongue and teeth do unimaginable things to her ear.

His hands have been busy too. Hardly noticing their efforts, Caroline finds herself almost naked. When he unclasps her bra and draws it down her arms, she holds her breath in anticipation of his touch.

But it isn't his hands that she feels; his tongue flicks over her nipples, wet and warm. His hands have moved on to other parts, her tanga briefs now on the floor at her feet.

With a fluid movement that takes Caroline completely unaware, Travis sweeps her off her feet and lays her gently on the bed.

Laughing she puts her arms out wide. "No hands see, now you're free to do as you will."

Moving over her, Travis kneels between her open legs and just looks at the woman before him. Naked and unashamed, she is his for the taking. But he wants her to experience love, not just sex.

"I love you, Caroline, with all my heart." He places a hand over her heart and feels its frantic beat. "Let me show you," he asks and bends to kiss her eyelids, then her cheeks and then her lips. "So kind...so caring... so beautiful," and punctuates each statement with a kiss to her body.

His hands are gentle and explore her with tender care. He wants to please Caroline, but more than that he wants to love her. When his hand moves down her leg her stomach tightens with expectation. But even though his hand skims up her inner thigh he doesn't touch her 'there'.

Instead he reaches out to her other leg, enjoying the feel of her soft skin. Again his hand moves up her inner thigh but by-passes the centre of her growing heat.

Moaning softly, Caroline tells him, "You're driving me crazy – you're torturing me."

His only answer is a dark smile before he dips his head to her belly and uses his tongue to good effect, causing her to cry out when he pushes in to the dip of her belly-button.

Her arms are no longer held out wide. Caroline has her fingers tangled in his beautiful long hair and holds him to her while he suckles at her breasts.

When his hand reaches down to cup her, Caroline almost falls apart, her breath hitches noisily and her hips lift to beg for more.

A single finger penetrates her wet heat and Travis moans with the pleasure of knowing he caused it. She wants him – this beautiful, generous woman really wants him.

Using his thumb on her clitoris at the same time, he delights in sending her over the first crest of passion. Her cries and moans are as much music to his ears as her skilful piano playing; only now he is in control.

"I want to kiss you at the heart of your womanhood," he tells her, and her eyes drift shut in anticipation. Just a single, breathy word slips between her lips, "Please."

His lips work from one knee up her inner thigh and then the other. Travis can feel her squirm her hips beneath him, desperate for him to reach her centre. When he does her moans of ecstasy are base and uncontrolled and he wants to hear more.

When he pushes his tongue inside her, Caroline obliges with a loud cry and bows her back off the bed as her body loses control again. Her climax is shockingly intense, and she falls back to the bed fighting for breath. But he doesn't stop.

His hands move beneath her buttocks and lift her to give him better access. Travis watches the effect that his tongue is having on his woman, looking down her body he can see her mouth fall open then her teeth clamp over her bottom lip.

He is hard as iron at the site of her, so responsive to his touch, to his love.

Lowering her hips he slowly enters her, watching as her breathing hitches and her whimpers build in to satisfying sighs of pleasure.

In and out, slow and deep, he holds himself back to give Caroline time to build again. When he feels her body begin to tense he thrusts harder and faster and is rewarded by a shriek so wild and uncontrolled that he too groans loudly with his release and the joy of feeling her tighten around him.

Travis! Wonderful, loving Travis...I adore you!

Wrapped in each other's arms and love, they fall into a blissfully contented sleep.

<u>Epilogue</u>

Erin Vandivier looks up at the lovely old house that sits back in a tree lined lane in an affluent part of the Midlands.

She hasn't really planned what she's going to say, but knows she has to do this. For too long she has kept Sara's secret, the consequences of which have come back to haunt her.

How could she have allowed a fine man like Tom to live his life thinking that he had done something wrong – that he was somehow to blame for his broken marriage?

It was wrong to stay silent then, and it would be wrong to stay silent now. Bracing herself for the worst, Erin walks up to the front door and knocks before she loses her nerve.

Alone in the hotel lounge, Caroline sits at the piano staring at the closed lid with trepidation in her heart. Looking down at her hands, still marked by fading bruises, she tentatively flexes her fingers.

What if they don't stretch and move as before? How can I live without my music?

Unknown to Caroline, Travis is watching from the shadows. No longer hiding himself away, he wants only to will her on but knows she won't try if she knows he is there.

Getting up, Caroline circles the piano, and then circles it again. Like weighing up an adversary, she contemplates its size and form, imagining the music she can draw out of it.

"I give you life!" Allowing her fingers to brush the smooth shiny lid, her sigh is like that of a lover. "And you give me such joy in return."

Taking her seat at the piano again, Caroline finally lifts the lid. Feeling an uncomfortable tingle in her hands she tries shaking them out at her sides. She knows it's just nerves, but her fear is very real.

Doing a few of the exercises that she learned during her physio sessions, Caroline starts to feel her fingers loosen up.

Closing her eyes she tries to imagine herself back on tour, the audience silently waiting for her to begin. Reaching out, her eyes still closed, Caroline holds her hands out to hover over the keys.

In her mind's eye she can see the keyboard, knows exactly where to begin. Her only problem is finding the nerve to do so.

When the first few notes sound, Caroline isn't sure; her reach is limited, her fingers stiffer than she is used to, but at least she is hitting the right notes.

"God Almighty, that was awful," she tells the empty room. "Bloody awful!"

Closing the lid, Caroline gets up and begins pacing. *I can't do it! I sound like I'm playing chopsticks with two fingers – what the hell am I going to do?*

In the shadows, Travis continues to will her on; desperate to step out and comfort her but knowing this is something Caroline needs to do alone.

"Ok, fine, so I'll play chopsticks!" And to Travis' great surprise that is exactly what she does.

Having made herself laugh, Caroline starts to relax. She doesn't attempt any serious pieces that require complete dexterity and sharp skills – instead she does a few simple exercises that she did in her childhood.

She is surprised and delighted that she even remembers them, but they are coming in useful now.

Travis finally feels he can leave her alone to find her way. Only Caroline would know what that way entails, after all, he'd just wanted to be close-by in case she became upset.

Tom is pacing the lounge of his hotel suite wondering where the hell Erin is. He went over to the Library and was told she had rung in sick. Thinking to check if she needed anything, he had gone to her house only to find it locked up tight with no signs of life inside.

He was sure he'd looked like a burglar casing the house when he had looked through the windows and called out to Erin through the letterbox. Tom hadn't wanted to ask the neighbours if they'd seen her in case she was taking a sickie in order to do other things. *How embarrassing would that be if she's only nipped out to the shops!*

"Damn it!" Pushing his hands back through his lush black hair, Tom decides to go back to Erin's house and see if she's back from the shops – "Or wherever the hell else!"

Logan has lent him the use of one of his company cars while he is in Sheriton and he uses it now to drive back over to Erin's. He doesn't even know why he is so worried about her, just that something is definitely not right.

All the way over to her house, Tom tries to think of places Erin might be. But there is a place he is reluctant to think about and he won't think about that until he has to.

"Shit!" he swore when she still wasn't home.

"Well, that's a nice hello, I'm sure," Erin speaks from behind him as she walks up the path.

Tom whizzes round and pulls her in to a tight embrace, shocking Erin then making her smile.

"What on earth is wrong?" she asks, tentatively returning his embrace.

When he steps back, Tom realises Erin is embarrassed and tries to apologise. "I'm sorry," he coughs somewhat embarrassed himself, "I think it's being back here...in Sheriton," he clarifies. "Old ghosts and bad memories." *Get a grip, man!*

Letting them both in to the house, Erin offers Tom a cup of tea. "Did you go to the library?" she asks nervously.

"I did, and you look remarkably well for someone on a sick day."

Erin actually blushes, something she hasn't done in years. But this man makes her feel foolish in so many ways – a woman of her age, too! *You should know better, Erin Vandivier! Much better!*

"I had to go on an urgent errand, a personal one," she tells him and turns to put the kettle on.

Deciding to push his luck, Tom asks, "Would that errand have anything to do with Sara's child?"

Erin doesn't answer or turn immediately, but continues until she has finished making their tea. Carrying it to the table she sits, contemplating the man seated opposite her.

Sara had loved him deeply. Whenever she spoke of Tom it was to praise him for his considerate ways and how good he was with the girls. She had never heard Sara complain about Tom, not even once.

When she drove him away, Erin knew it was the hardest thing Sara had ever done – until the day she gave away her new born baby. That had almost killed her; her grief locked up inside so as not to affect Catherine. But it had taken its toll; Sara had lost weight and rather than become listless and lifeless she had thrown herself in to working, even if it was just around the house. She needed to be exhausted to sleep; she had told Erin when she'd voiced her concerns. And so it had gone on, until finally Sara buried her shame and loss and got on with life.

"She never even looked at another man," Erin spoke softly. "Sara loved you till the day she died – I'm just sorry that I was a part of letting you think otherwise." Her eyes are caste down, staring in to her tea.

"I don't blame you, Erin. And I don't blame Sara, come to that," he assures her. "It was a bad time all around; Sara dealt with it the only way she knew how – my regret is that she didn't trust me to stand by her...and the child."

Heaving a sigh of relief, Erin reaches across the table to place a comforting hand over Tom's.

"It wasn't that she didn't trust you," she corrects him earnestly. "It was the shame, the horror of what had been done to her. Sara wouldn't have told me but for the fact that I called round on the same day that it happened and she was in too much of a state to hide it."

Taking a gulp of air, Tom's chest tightens painfully at the thought of what had been done to Sara. "Did she know him?" he asks quietly, but Erin can hear the undertone of anger in Tom's voice.

"I...I...she didn't tell me." Erin is warring with her conscience and her growing feelings for Tom. "I had my suspicions, but Sara never confirmed them."

"Did she deny them?" he asks suddenly eager. But Erin hesitates, worrying that she might be wrong and the consequences of that could be truly awful. "Erin...?" his voice isn't soft or gentle anymore, but demanding and urgent.

"Thomas Thornton, don't you raise your voice to me," she tells him quietly but very firmly. "Just give me time to think – if I'd had any proof back then don't you think I'd have reported him to the police; even anonymously to spare Sara?"

"Damn it!" Getting up, Tom can't think straight – his Sara, his wife and mother to his children was raped in their own home almost certainly by someone she knew and no doubt trusted. "Oh fuck it!" Tom sinks down into an easy chair in the breakfast room adjoining the kitchen and cries as never before.

Erin is shocked and hurt to see his pain, and more than ever regrets her part in causing it.

Realising this is the first time Tom has grieved for the loss of Sara and for the loss of their life together; Erin moves to sit beside him on the arm of the chair. Handing him a box of tissues she waits, her arm across his shoulders, for the storm to pass.

Till now, Tom had thought that Sara didn't want him or love him, to find out different is too much to keep inside. His mind is full of 'what if's'. What if he hadn't moved away but had waited near-by; would she have come to him eventually? Would they have worked through the problems and stayed together, if so, might she not now be dead?

A knock at the front door causes them both to jump and Tom quickly dries his face and blows his nose, trying desperately to pull himself together.

"I'll get rid of whoever it is," she rubs Tom's back then gets up to answer the door.

"Sorry to disturb but we went to the library and they..."

"This is not a good time," Erin interrupts Caroline mid flow. "I have a visitor, you'll have to come back another day," then Erin makes to close the door.

"It's alright," Tom calls out from the back room, "they have a right to know what's going on."

Reluctantly, Erin steps back to allow Caroline and Catherine to enter. Looking straight at Catherine she lowers her voice to a harsh whisper, "Don't you dare go in there and upset your dad," she warns. "It would do you good to remember that's just who he is, your dad, and that he has feelings, too!"

Having come here with the idea of trying to intimidate more information out of Erin, Catherine is surprised to find that it is she who is intimidated. The trouble with that is her defensive reflex.

"Don't get in my face," she bites out shoving her own face right up to Erin's, and would have said more but Caroline quickly steps in.

"Ok, cool it!" Caroline demands. "Let's just go and see dad and find out what's going on!"

The pair of them gasp at the sight of him. Caroline rushes forward to kneel in front of him, and even Catherine can't help moving forward to sit nearby.

"Dad, what is it? What's been going on?" Caroline asks, and does a good impression of Catherine when she glares up at Erin.

"It isn't Erin's fault," he tells them quickly. "I just got upset talking about your mum."

Catherine frowns but listens more closely.

"But why…" Caroline asks mystified, "…you never have before?"

Reaching forward, Tom strokes a gentle hand down his daughter's cheek. "Not in front of you, no…but alone…at night…"

Wrapping her arms around his neck, Caroline hugs him tightly. "You're not alone," she rebukes him, "you never have been." *I didn't know. Never guessed. Oh, dad!*

Erin has been busy in the kitchen making more tea. Carrying a tray through to the sitting room she asks them to join her.

It takes a minute or two for everyone to settle and be served a cup of tea – Erin uses this time to collect her thoughts and courage to say what she now knows she has to.

"I've been to see your sister's parents," she tells her audience of three, all looking startled at her news. "That's where I went this morning," she tells Tom, and he nods at her confirmation of his suspicion.

"Sister, you know that for sure?" Catherine asks, quietly for her.

"I do…now," she explains. "Until this morning I was as much in the dark about that as you. Her parents, however, were happy to provide at least that little information." *I just wish I had better news.* "Unfortunately, that was all they would tell me, but they did say they would contact their daughter and ask her to come home as soon as possible – then they'll discuss it with her and give her the choice of what happens next."

"So what now…who are they…do they live locally…?" Catherine is up and pacing now, her thoughts racing. Another young girl, her sister, has grown up thinking she wasn't wanted. *Well, I'll soon fix that! Fuck! Fuck! Fuck!*

Caroline goes to her sister, hating the torment so obviously tearing at her. "It's alright, Catherine, we'll find her and let her know that we're here for her if she wants to meet us."

"Fuck that!" she explodes, and Caroline wishes Logan were here. But it's their dad who takes control.

"Stop that!" he demands, standing to face Catherine. "I know you're frightened for her – that she'll feel like you, abandoned, and unwanted by anyone who matters!" he states bluntly. "But you are so wrong," Tom tells her more gently. "When your mother died I tried to get you back…"

"Liar!" she shouts, not wanting to hear this.

"No, I'm not," he insists, but Tom isn't sure that he can get through to Catherine after all these years of her being alone. "They told me that you were too traumatised to meet me after not knowing me for so long. They said that, in all probability, it would damage you further to be taken by a stranger to a home and a sister you didn't know."

Her head is slowly shaking, but Catherine can hear the truth behind his words. "You…you came for me – you really came for me…?"

Caroline is stood to one side against the wall, tears spilling down her face.

"I never wanted to leave you in the first place," he tells her, walking to stand inches in front of Catherine but not daring to reach out. "I've thought of you and your mum a million times every day without exception. I love you, Catherine, I always have!"

Without thought or embarrassment, Catherine flings herself in to his arms and weeps in great gulping sobs. "Oh, daddy," are the only two coherent words he can make out, but Tom couldn't be happier to hear them.

"We'll find her, Catherine," and he strokes her hair while hugging her to him. *And this time no one will stand in my way! God help anyone who tries!*

*****

I hope you have enjoyed this book, if so please take the time to write a review at the place of purchase.

Susan Elle